Homes of Healing
Part 3

The Writers Retreat

Olwyn Harris

Published by: Reading Stones Publishing
                  Helen Brown & Wendy Wood
                  www.woodwendy1982.wixsite.com/readingstones

Cover Design: Wendy Wood

For more copies, contact the publisher at:

Glenburnie Homestead
212 Glenburnie Road
ROB ROY NSW 2360
Mobile: 0422 577 663
Email: hbrown19561@gmail.com

Dedication

For all those who have said to me over the years, "you should write a book". Your words have built up my courage to take the risk and share my stories with others.

1.

He handed me the keys. "It's out of the way though. Keys are a bit of a token. The windows and door by the laundry don't lock. You okay with that?"

"I was looking for out-of-the-way."

"Well like I said, we haven't done much more than replace the roof. It is really rough. There's water, power, and just basic furniture. That's about it." Ray handed me a sheet with essential local information.

I hadn't heard a sale's pitch that refreshingly honest in a while. "Well… I'm happy to sign for six months, but if it turns out to be too much for me how about I pay a fortnight now, and then weekly in advance? That way I can move on if it doesn't work out." He looked at me as though I was probably an axe murderer, so I tried to sound reassuring. "Really, this sounds like exactly what I was wanting. I'll come down on Tuesdays and pay for the coming week."

He didn't hesitate when I handed him the cash amount. "Sure. The Missus will be home. Or you can leave the rent in the canister by the hall lamp if she's out."

"Okay." Axe murderer or not, he was not going to begin a Cultural Revolution and start locking up.

I followed the track up over the hill. The hut was out of sight and could have been a thousand miles into the wilderness. It was equipped with power, good mobile reception, a bed, and a table. Space. Quiet. Nature. What else did I need? Nothing. It was perfect. I had no doubt this little out-of-the-way stone hut had a story. It was my job to find it.

5

A common response when people discover I'm a writer, is to say that they also have a book inside them waiting to be written. To me it often seems to be less about the story they had to tell, and more about having pages in print with their name on the cover. Then there were the fellow-writers who'd talk about taking a sabbatical to devote to their craft, and still end up squeezing it in at the end of a day crammed with corporate business and professional grind, years later. I felt a glow of satisfaction that I wasn't just talking about this. I was doing it. Really doing it.

I found Rocky Creek Farm Stay on the Internet, and when I made enquiries, the owners very apologetically confessed their projected timelines had not been met. Somehow the listing had not been withdrawn. But I was really taken with the rustic aspect of the photo and appealed to them to let it to me anyway. More like a trial let. Basic made it cheaper.

The key opened the front door. The building had an internal wall that divided off an area for the bedroom. The laundry-toilet had a very basic rose-head shower fitting that attached to a garden hose on one of the taps. I unloaded the boxes I had brought with me, made up the bed with my linen and unstacked my set of crockery and pans. They had acquired a rather rickety second-hand freestanding stove and a bench of sorts that served as the kitchenette. The sink was a plastic basin with a draining rack on a tray. It was evident from my conversation over the phone that their plans were for a well-appointed, comfortable retreat, but just now it was a very honest assessment to say it was rudimentary.

I had allowed myself a margin of settling-in before I would begin writing but, as my few boxes were unpacked, I found the freshness of the air and the simplicity of the setting had me bursting to start. My love is historical romance, and this place was the perfect backdrop for fiery conflicts and tender resolutions involving long skirts and patched britches held up with braces.

When I plied Ray's wife for some information on the history of the farm, she looked really vague. They had bought the property eight years ago, but they showed very little curiosity regarding its history. Perhaps a more fruitful source of information might be the locals. Sandra pointed me in the direction of the farm cemetery that was located up on a rocky rise. An old quarry had been worked on the farm at some point, and she offered the name of the local historical society co-ordinator. It felt like a jigsaw: a box full of random pieces without a picture to help put it together. But then it dawned on me, I actually I did have the picture; I had the stone hut. Now I had to work out how it fitted together. How much would be truth, fiction and creative license? I realised a while ago I am not too loyal to the accuracy of local legends. That was the advantage, or the curse, of not being 'local'. I just wanted to find my story.

I sat down at the old timber table with my computer and waited. I looked up at the old slab beams above me, willing them to speak part of the story they had witnessed over the years. It's usually how I start. Soaking myself in place and space, being present to the characters as I allow them to introduce themselves… to share their dilemmas and watch their story unfold. I've always taken the stance that I am a custodian of the character and their story. It is never mine to own or manipulate. My responsibility is to be faithful to document their story as it unfolds.

2

I closed the lid to my computer and got up and walked to the door. I shaded my eyes and then grabbed my hat and I walked out over the paddocks, past sheep grazing lazily, towards the cemetery. I stood and looked around. Weeds and thistles were the only flowers that offered these headstones any colour. They were weathered and cracked, but I took photos of each one, and tried to imagine how these people fitted together in their common experience of this place. More of the jigsaw. There were a couple of names that stood out for me. And a baby. The dates indicated he had died at birth. How were they all connected? What was life... and death... like here all those years ago? Were they subject to disease, droughts, fires, and floods? What about bushrangers and crime? The research I had done uncovered a couple local convictions of stagecoach robberies. The area had an established history of sheep farming. It was my style to mix that up, and instead of sheep, I imagined a cattle duffing outfit tracking over these paddocks stealing prized stock. A few tell-tale corner posts remained, covered in grass and vines. Were these the corner-stays for the holding yards where owners had stood protectively over their animals? The day was warming quickly as I walked back. The sun reflected off the gravel track and shimmered white in the morning light. I stood in the doorway and wondered what had drawn these people to this place?

Suddenly I felt form and shape embody those names on the stones, eroded from the weather. A beautiful young woman burst in on my study and I saw her storm around the room in frustration. As I watched, the history faded, and the story emerged. Part of the fun is not having to worry about how accurate my tale is. I choose names to match the characters as they introduce themselves to me. It also soothes the distress of local historical fanatics who find my use of fictional license too disloyal to be tolerated. But this is my process; this is how I do what I do. I ask questions and allow the story to answer the puzzle. How did they end up here? As I watched this woman pace backwards and forwards, I instinctively knew this was Magdalena... Meg. I also knew Meg was independent and fierce in an era where women were usually supported and compliant. What had it cost her to be here? Why was she alone? What was her relationship with her neighbours? If she had worked so hard to achieve a certain level of independence, what was her drive, her motivation? Was it just survival, or was there more that stoked that fire in her belly? Why was the house where I saw my heroine pace up and down, a colonial style timber cottage with a verandah? My little hut was made of stone. That didn't add up. In my mind, this little writer's retreat had definitely been Meg's place as well.

I loved the mystery of being able to ask these questions. Of exploring the community and the region just to feel how it might have felt to be there with them. Of not knowing who these people were yet or what had brought them to this particular place. It held a kind of obsessive anticipation for me as I waited to learn more about them and what they had gone through. Sometimes I found these answers in local records; some of it fell onto the page as I wrote. The frustration of not having tidy answers and clear plots is part of the way their storytelling unfolds for me. After all, it is their story. They have the right to allow it to be messy if that is the way it is.

My reflections were interrupted by a ute driving up along the track. Ray pulled up in a cloud of dust and waved apologetically as he wound down the window. "I know you said you were coming down later with the rent, but I wanted to catch you and run something by you. I've gotta go out later."

"Oh. Fair enough. I'll get it for you." I turned inside and grabbed my wallet. Did he think I would forget? Anyway, the sooner I gave him what he came for, the quicker I could return to my musings. I counted out the notes and he wrote a receipt with the pad held up against the steering wheel. I took the receipt, but he made no move to go.

"Um, well, the Missus and I wanted to check something with you. It's just that with you being here, we are kinda keen to get going on with the original plan… you know: having the Bed-and-Breakfast all set up."

"You want me to vacate?" I had just paid for another week!

"No. No! We were hoping that you'll stay on 'cause that is mighty helpful for us. But Sandra was thinking that with the money you are paying, we can put that directly back into the place. We want to get it all fixed up while you're here so that it'll be ready to list properly when you're done. You've got it for as long as you need though… we wanted you to be sure about that."

I sort of thought he had to be kidding. Why would I give permission to disturb my quiet, out-of-the-way writing retreat, to have it overrun with tradesmen, so they could put up the rent? It didn't sound like there was any benefit at all for me in

11

this plan. Instead I calmly asked, "So what exactly are you thinking that might entail?"

"Well, we'd just do projects as we get enough money for each part. You know what you pay, so it certainly isn't going to be quick by any means." Huh. That was unnecessary. "But we've got enough to start the bathroom and laundry, so we reckon it's only fair you have hot water and a shower at least. Thought we'd start with that and go on from there. Maybe the kitchenette next. What do you think?"

Okay. Right. That was my immediate payoff: hot water, a shower, and a washing machine. Trips to the Laundromat would be over. That was his trump card. "Well, I want your word: no increases in rent while I'm here... at least for six months. And if you can limit the trade-work to three weekdays, I'll make myself scarce on those days." I should have asked for a discount – inconvenience allowance.

He grinned, amiably. "See. I said to the Missus, we can only ask the question. I know it ain't the most done thing to be asking a tenant this... and it's not like we have the history of being mates to draw on, but it will benefit you too, making things a little more comfy while you're stay'n here. Least, that was my thinking. We're grateful that you're being so accommodating about it. The brother-in-law has had some terrible strife at his place, so he's going to stay with us for a bit. He's handy with the practical things, so he's going to do the work for us. It'll help him out some too. We're not expecting to start until next fortnight or so, but I'll let you know anyhow."

He waved and left in another cloud of dust. Two weeks reprieve. It hardly seemed enough.

I went back inside and made myself a coffee. He had said I was being amiable about it, but in truth I was annoyed by the interference. This was supposed to be my space, my terms, and already it was being imposed upon. Not that I begrudged them their dream. It's just that I wasn't counting on catering to other people's plans just yet. The whole idea of removing myself from my normal world was so that I didn't have to constantly hanker after everyone else's needs. This was my dream... in a very unapologetic egocentric, narcissistic, selfish way. My space, my agenda, my timetable, my itinerary. I wanted the freedom not to have to accommodate other people's ideas, programs, roles, objectives – however worthwhile, because, let's face it, even when I attended to every detail with fastidious care, it was rarely appreciated anyway.

Writing is a very alone world for me. Suddenly I held a new respect for those who were able to block out spaces in a normal, busy life and make it happen. The discipline required in achieving that deserved my admiration. I looked out the window and sighed. Maybe I hadn't found the distraction-free zone I had hoped for by coming here after all. Maybe I had just transposed myself to a new place, with new set of people, with their own particular agendas, expectations and impositions.

3.

How did Meg handle the intrusions in her life? How did a single woman survive in an isolated world without a backup plan? Even something with a simple enough objective would become complicated as she tried to counter the logistics of isolation, and the barriers of a society where women were treated with scorn, or if you were lucky, mere condescension. I left Meg considering her options with the problems that crowded her life, and drove myself into town.

I needed to find a library or café or some place with Internet where I could go on Ray's renovation days to write. Once I would have probably sat cramped and sweaty in my car with my laptop because I generously offered to accommodate someone else's repairs. But now I was inclined to be kind to myself. After all, I was here to write so I needed an option that supported that with at least some level of ease. I tried the library... but it was only open till lunchtime... and every second Saturday morning. Of course. The limitations of Rural-Remote. I asked if they knew of any office space or rooms in town that hired on a daily rate. They looked at me blankly. I figured it might have been more reasonable to expect an international flight from their little country aerodrome. The café in town was small and dingy and smelt like stale fried fish oil. All the appeal of vomit in the back of your throat. The woman behind the counter wiped her hands on her grubby apron and grunted at my enquiry with an equally grubby attitude. She didn't have seating to spare, which was reserved for eating customers.

I was wondering how I could renege on my hasty agreement to make the apartment available for renovations. Of course, I called the shell of a shed 'an apartment'. It sounded so much more… 'writers-retreat'. I was starving and there was no way I was eating in that café, so I hightailed it for the pub. Inside was dim and cool and I looked at the menu board and I placed my order, including a coffee. The barman smiled. That put me at ease. "Hi. My name is Tess. Who would I speak to about using one of the tables during the day?"

"That'd be me," he said. "Barman, proprietor, kitchen-hand, manager, janitor. My name is Theo."

"I'm looking for a place to work a couple of days during the week. I offered to vacate where I'm staying to allow for renovations, but I hit an unexpected glitch in my plan because the library isn't open after lunch."

"Oh… you're the writer from Ray's place." He looked kind of amused, like I was a novelty ride in side-show alley. Or perhaps he thought it was more like a freak show.

I tried to make my presence sound as inconspicuous as possible, with the benefit of orders of regular coffee and meals. He let me rattle on for a while. "Sure. Pick a table that suits you. I'll make sure no one bothers you. You can stay as long as you want." And he wrote down the password to his Wi-Fi. At least I could retain the dignity of being a person of my word, and let Ray and Sandra get on with their renovations. Hopefully it would mean a properly installed shower and a functioning washing machine in the not too distant future.

4.

On Tuesday Ray wanted to get started on some preparations before the brother-in-law arrived to start work on the bathroom, so I evacuated to Delacey's Pub and settled myself into a corner with a cappuccino and toast. As promised, Theo did not disturb me, and I saw a couple of patrons raise an eyebrow or arch their forehead in my direction. I've no idea what he told them, but they scowled, nodded and went back to their drinks and snacks and phones with only the occasional dubious look in my direction. I soon got an idea of who were regular patrons, who were sometimes-customers and those who were just passing through.

I found a comfortable routine, undisturbed by the banter at the bar, fuelled by Ramon's incredible dishes that were disguised as simple country fare on the menu board, and Theo's coffees. I clicked away at my keyboard. One afternoon, just after lunchtime, a retired-aged couple came in. They sat down, evidently expecting table service with no inclination to accommodate a country pub's skeleton staff by ordering at the bar. Theo went over to them and they immediately started abusing him in a foreign language. He stared at them tolerantly, poured some table-water. He came over to me while they looked at the menu and topped up my glass as well. "Hey, would you mind if I talk to them?" I asked quietly.

"Don't know why you would want to, but feel free," he said rolling his eyes.

I stood up, picked up my notepad beside my computer and then went to their table. I apologised to them in Italian and said I had been on a break. When I asked where they were from, they looked relieved and we chatted for a while. They were on a holiday to visit his cousin and thought that they would take a scenic route. They were shocked by Australian distances and were overwhelmed by the heat. They were obviously exhausted and hungry. I explained the menu and took their order and, as I gave it to Theo, I quietly asked him, "So when was this place originally built? And give me one of your best Barossa Reds..." I went back to their table and pointed to the humble bar. "This Australian 'pub' – public-house, was built in the mid 1800's. In Australian terms it is quite old. In Italy it would be just a bambino." I asked if they wanted to try something Australian. "You can tell me how it compares with your Italian wines," I said as I poured them a taster. Like wine connoisseurs they swirled and inhaled the aroma and sipped the bouquet discerningly. They nodded and approved and still graded their Italian wines much higher. To be expected. But they said that they would have a glass with their meal and take a bottle to their cousin and tell him of this little Australian pub experience. Theo was grinning as he handed me their dishes and it spurred me on to explain to them that the cuisine was fresh produce from local industry. I was pretty confident the only 'local' aspect to their meals was the delivery made from the supermarket down the street, but I sold a pretty good yarn. I am a storyteller after all.

I went back and stood behind the bar like I owned it. Theo turned away so that they couldn't see the smirk on his face. As he dried glasses, I picked up a cloth and wiped down the bar, and then went and cleaned some of the tables over and adjusted some chairs. When they were ready for the check, I took it to them, and they paid, adding a generous tip. I graciously said I hoped that their air-conditioning held out for the rest of their outback Australian road-trip. They had relaxed, were a little refreshed and went on their way with a generous all enveloping hug from la Mamma. I handed the money to Theo. He pushed the tip back. "Think you earned that. Obviously, you've done that before."

"No, actually I have never worked in a pub." I chuckled. "They were just tired and hot and hungry and out of the familiar." I shrugged. "We could sort some of those for them."

"You speak Italian."

"A bit. Not well. Helps to know basics... booking accommodation and stuff for clients."

I went back to my corner and settled in with the complimentary coffee Theo made for me. He even added a dash of hazelnut. That had felt good. What I had enjoyed more than the customers' smile was being comfortable enough to help out. It had the incredible feeling of belonging. And I noticed that Theo was secure enough to accept it. The tip was not too shabby either. It was energising and I wrote a good solid couple of pages without pause.

The next week, in the quiet lull of the afternoon, Theo came over with a couple of coffees and asked if he could sit. I closed the lid to my lap-top and laughed about being so jacked up on caffeine I'd had trouble sleeping since I started inhabiting the Delacey precinct.

Theo shrugged and observed he thought that was a better look than being rolling drunk. "What you did when that couple came in the other day... that was music. I enjoyed watching that."

"Well thank you Sir. I do like to think that providing entertainment for the staff is one of the benefits of being a part-time tenant of your corner."

He grinned. "I was just wondering... since you are here, if you would help out when there's stuff going on... if there are things that need doing?"

I blinked. Another intrusion on my space. But I firmly reminded myself, this actually wasn't my space. It was his. Perhaps he was territorially marking out the boundaries, like a man-dog. Wouldn't want me to forget my place. Suddenly the joy of helping out was being translated into obligation. Perhaps my time here was done, and I should just go down to the café. Cramped. Grumpy. Grimy. That was a less than an appealing option. Nope. Would prefer not.

"How much would I need to do before I could sit out?"

"Depends on what needs doing. You track your hours. No point trying to find something to do for the sake of it. Thursdays we have some regular business bookings, so lunch is busier. If there's nothing going on you can go back to your... Oh." His grin faded. "You think I want you to do this for the privilege of sitting in my corner," he accused me.

I shrugged. What could I say? I did think that.

"Of course, I'm going to pay you. Award. I just lost one of my casual staff that's all. And tips are yours – if you can get them, which doesn't seem to be an issue." His voice had a defensive edge.

19

My routine was interrupted anyway by having to vacate and come here. And a paying job, which didn't require too much imagination actually sounded helpful: really helpful. I was protectively guarding my creativity, but I was also mindful of the reality that my financial reserve was not an eternal giving tree. "My apologies for misreading the offer. You are right: I am already here… so why not? I trust you won't be too disappointed if all my customer encounters don't turn out like poetry. I have told you quite honestly: I really have no hospitality experience."

He didn't even pause. "Noted and acknowledged. I'll give you a walk around while there's not much going on."

On the way home after that first day's work I went for a drive to just get out into countryside and I sort of lost track of time. It was dark when I opened the door and turned on the light. I threw my car keys in the bowl on the table and went to the fridge to see what I could manage for a light supper.

"Good evening, Miss Forrester."

I jumped a mile. Grief! I spun around. A stranger was sitting on my lounge. I looked for something in self-defence and scrambled for a knife near the kitchen basin.

He stood up apparently oblivious to the distress he was causing. "I stayed to introduce myself. I'm Keith, Sandra's brother. I am working on your bathroom and shower."

"I don't care who you are, or what you're working on. After five it is my home again. You have no right to be here."

Sandra seemed normal enough. Was her brother a completely deranged closet-kept family secret?

"Huh. Ray said you were being right obliging about all this. You don't seem as friendly as he said you would be."

"I'm not responsible for him misrepresenting my demeanour." Keith blinked and stammered. And it occurred to me, I might have used big words too complicated for his basic vocabulary. That was an indicator of what I was dealing with here. I dumbed it down: "Go away! Sitting in the dark, in my living room is properly creepy. Get out! You are not welcome."

He didn't even blink, but raised his eyebrows and picked up the electric jug and plugged it in. "I thought we might have a cup of tea," he said eagerly, "since I'm fixing up your place." He spoke as if that was the logical next step in this bizarre behaviour.

"Are you serious?" The man was one-hundred-percent disturbing.

"It would be a real bummer if the bathroom did not turn out as nicely as you hoped."

"Is that supposed to be a threat? This is not my house. Talk to Ray about the quality of your work. It has nothing to do with me. Now get out!"

He seemed quite bewildered that I wasn't inviting him to dinner with a heart bubbling over with gratitude. I showed him the door and he stammered incoherently obviously still hoping for demonstrations of misplaced indebtedness. I locked the front door and wedged a chair against the back door when he left. Nutter!

I worked with Theo effortlessly. 'Easy going' was his signature. I had my list of things to do, and got in and did extra chores that needed attending to. It was not hard work and the anticipated Thursday rush of customers was short lived. He was quick to give me a 'staff discount' on meals and drinks, and there was still that flow of complimentary left-over orders that found their way to my corner when I had time to sit and write. Most afternoons I managed a couple of hours to myself. Theo would bring me a coffee, and sometimes he'd sit for a few minutes and chat.

One day he said to me, "I wasn't actually looking to hire. Sure, the casual opening was there but I usually don't like who I end up with. But this time, I gotta say, I'm really glad you've come. We have a nice rhythm."

I smiled. That was pleasant – to be appreciated. And surprising. I would have thought he'd have people lining up for a job. I knew enough of the local climate to realise opportunities were not overly abundant. I felt fortunate to have found a casual job with such ease. The work was uncomplicated and that was appealing. Theo seemed uncomplicated and that was also appealing. "How could you not have successful hires? You're the easiest person I've ever worked for."

"Hmm. Well of course I have my regular staff. But this is a small town. I think most try out, not because they want a job, but because they want a boyfriend. So, although you think I'm easy, I've brushed off so many offers it's got to the point where there's this general assumption around town that I've got a thing going with my cook. Albeit, he is a very good cook."

22

"Do you?"

"Do I what?"

"Have a thing with your cook?"

He smiled, and then paused. "Does it matter?"

"Well it does if I want to know if I'm in for a chance. I might want to join the queue." I laughed. He didn't really seem to be the type who had tickets on himself. Perhaps I was wrong.

His eyes sort of crinkled in the most disarming way. "Never had that as a comeback. Cute."

"Huh. Who's cute? You've just told me you have people lining up for a job to get to you. That's pretty confident. Or arrogant."

"I work in a pub. I see just about everything imaginable. Women come in here with makeup and pheromones caked on and leave with anyone. Men do the same... generally without the makeup, but not always. I can tell when someone is on the hunt. It doesn't strike me that you are."

"What makes you so sure I'm not 'on the hunt'? I could be... stealthy." It was a good-humoured exchange. I was quite amused that he did not seem at all uncomfortable, talking about that awkward territory of relationships. Perhaps because relationships are a study of mine, I was interested in his perspective.

"You sit here in your corner in your jeans with your coffee. You notice, but avoid eye-contact. You choose when you take bathroom breaks, so you miss bumping into people. I've seen you shut people down when they've tried to chat you up. Stuff like that."

"Frumpy and isolated. That's not flattering."

23

"I didn't say frumpy. I might have said 'content', which is different. I thought you must have had someone. That you want to know whether you're 'in for a chance' surprises me."

I didn't want to talk about me, so I deflected. "What's your story then, if the general consensus is that you and the cook are a happy couple?"

He looked at me for a while as if considering something. "We'd been here around about six years, eight months, a week and four days when my ex decided to tell me this was never part of her ten-year plan."

"Approximately…"

"There abouts. And yes, I was completely sideswiped. As they say: never saw it coming. I call it my summer-from-hell, and that is not just alluding to the heatwave we had that year. I thought we were in it together. I thought it was about us, and not location or occupations or timelines, but apparently not. Just like that. I got the family pub. She got the house back in the suburbs and the dog. That was our 50-50 split."

"And so, you let the rumour persist that you left her for the cook? That is generous."

"No one has ever called it generous before."

"Doesn't sound like you go out of your way to clarify whether it was generous or not."

"It's convenient probably. They leave me alone."

"And what about the guys? Do they hit on you?"

"Sometimes, but this is a conservative community. And I don't date customers. If they are here, they are customers."

"What about Ramon? Does he mind?"

"Ramon is gay. He sees his partner on his days off; he lives a couple of hours away. Ramon is cool about it. Amused probably. He says it builds his reputation."

"Well it is an interesting little world you've created for yourself here, Theo."

"It does okay."

"Content?" I asked and looked him in the eye. Hazel with a tinge of sadness I thought.

"Hmm. Maybe. Familiar anyway."

"Sometimes that works too." And then a customer called him away for service.

5.

I sat looking over the paddocks. The low trees were swaying their olive-grey leaves in the breeze, bent by the ravages of the elements, and harsh environment, making do and surviving. I couldn't get Theo's disclosure out of my mind. It stayed with me and tormented me with questions I had never asked before. What would a love look like if it didn't come with conditions and provisos? How would that sort of love behave if a couple were in it together? What would a love be if it was not about location or occupations or timelines or misfortunes? It seemed inevitable. When the starry-eyed idealism of romance collapses, when faced with the stuff of ordinary life, or unexpected tragedies, or the allure of status, or ideas of progress, was it inevitable that love digresses, and togetherness becomes irretrievably diverted? Was it possible to love someone, as Theo believed, based on being together through the rough, not dependent on a timeline of accumulating the appropriate amount of junk or hitting the calculated number of home runs?

Then there was a bigger question. Did I have the capacity to love like that? Would it always end up in pain, regardless of how idealistic it started out? It struck me how unsatisfactory it was that romantic stories rarely finish the tale, but only acknowledged the journey together has started. That had never been an issue for me before. This is what I did. I worked at getting my characters to find each other, see past their flaws and into bed. But what about the rest of their lives? What happens when they realise their life goals are heading off in completely different directions? What do you do with an epiphany that comes after six years, eight months, a week and four days that changes the way you see everything? Does that automatically mean there is nothing left to warrant being together? What keeps people true to those ideals when the harshness of life and the pain of reality kicks in? Because it always will. Always. The reality of those weather-beaten trees stood stark in my vision. Each one of those trees was once a supple and straight sapling, full of potential and promise, and now they stood bent and scarred and old. The elements of nature had not been kind. Would love always end up worn, twisted, bitter, condemned?

"Something's going on." Theo put down two coffees and a plate of some amazing Ramon pasta creation. He was not at all shy about sitting down opposite me. I noticed that. That felt like belonging too. The freedom to just be there.

I looked up from my computer. I was playing solitaire. "Like what?"

"Like the contentment has become restless."

"Mr Delacey, are you performance managing me by telling me in a round-about way that my work ethic is slipping?"

"Not your ethics, but perhaps the poise. If working here does not suit you then why don't you just go back to writing stories?"

"Are you sacking me?"

"Of course not. It's just that you seem… distracted maybe. I don't want to be the cause of that."

"Theo…" I picked up my fork and played with the food on my plate. "You're right. I'm not writing. Distracted is spot on."

"Hmm. Figured. But not in a good way. Right?"

"Would you mind if I told you something? Friend to friend?"

He looked grave. "Well I take such a role very… Sorry. You are not in the mood to be teased. Sure. Spill away. I'll add 'confidant' to the list of things I do."

Perhaps I was taking it too far. Perhaps I had no reason to be annoyed and disturbed and downright freaked out by Keith's unrelenting, obsessive, weird attachment. But as I spoke, and the more I described what had been going on at my little cottage, Theo's face became increasingly sober. By the time I had finished it clouded in a storm.

"You do know there is a word for this? Criminal stalking! You have every right to be concerned. It should be reported."

"I don't want to report it. I've spoken to Ray about it. He said he'll sort it, but he keeps making excuses for him. He thinks that since Keith is on the rebound, he just needs some time to get it together. But I'm at the point, where I don't even care that his heart has been broken. It creeps me out!"

"Friend to friend… right?"

"That's what I asked for."

"Can a friend get involved then?"

"In what way?"

"Well. I would like permission to firmly remind Ray that he needs to keep his workers in check, even if they are family. Especially if they are getting their love-lives sorted. You know…" He stopped, unfinished.

"I know what? What else?"

"Tess, if you don't want to go back there tonight, you know you can stay here. I have rooms. Any one of them is yours if you just say so... worker's rates; first night free. Or..."

I was grateful that he would not minimise or belittle my concern. But I didn't want to run. I wanted my plan to work. I didn't want to relinquish my retreat because an unsettling individual with a disturbing psychological bent had taken on renovating the bathroom suite. "Or? Please tell me you think there is another option..."

"I'm guessing by the way you hesitate, staying here is not your preferred course of action."

"I'd be running." I shrugged. "It just seems drastic to evacuate just yet."

"I was thinking there is something else we could try..." He faded out, reluctant to proceed.

"If you have some other alternative here that could be helpful... please. I appreciate any input." I eagerly coaxed him on.

"Well, just as an observation: it seems this Keith thinks you are fair game because you're single. You said that a couple of times... him harping on your status."

"Yeah – it seems wrong to him. It's probably more that he is now single, and he considers that wrong." I looked at him curiously.

He cleared his throat in an uncomfortable sort of way. "So... I was thinking about what you said that time I told you about my ex. About this constructed world that I have made that keeps unhelpful people out of my way."

"Oh. The cook."

29

"Well. What if you had your own cook? Keith might buy it."

"Ramon?"

"Not sure Ramon would be convincing enough in this scenario, even though it's pretty obvious to me Keith has a kangaroo or two loose in the top paddock."

Even in the serious, he offered relief. I grabbed the idea and the reprieve with both hands and chuckled. When he gestured self-consciously, I couldn't help but be charmed. "Oh, I see." I considered his bashful offer with a smile.

"Could you trust me in this? It is a big responsibility."

"Hmm. This is also generous. You think you can pull off being my cook. If nothing else, to see how you will do that is amusing enough to secure my buy in. You're on."

I rattled the key in the door. There was no way to predict if Keith would be there sitting in the dark, or be lurking somewhere else, or… not here at all. One evening I found him on the toilet; another time cooking dinner; or hand washing my tea-towels. Theo had his arm reassuringly around my waist and we braced ourselves with a prepared laugh as we walked in.

Theo sort of nodded to me as he spotted a shadow sitting on the lounge. I expected him to burst on the light and scream obscenities at him, instead he pulled me closer and whispered, "You okay? See if you can go with this…" He cupped his hand behind my neck, and I felt a shiver. I wasn't sure if it was his or mine. I stiffened as I felt his body come close and wondered if I was trading one type of intrusion for another. I could see

Theo was thinking. He murmured something meaningless, and then loud enough to be heard, he said we needed a drink. He pulled me over towards the fridge. In the light of the open door, positioned so Keith could have no doubt who we were and what we were doing, he again gently placed his hand in the arc of my neck and drew me in for a kiss. Suddenly I felt myself responding, so subtly, so unconsciously. It was a suspended moment and I wanted to linger in the headiness of the arms of a man who was caring for me in this moment. I had no intention of noticing it was a fabricated moment.

Gradually he released me and coughed. He looked at me seriously and said, "Tess, Honey… don't freak out, but I think there is a man in your living room."

The spell was broken. "Oh what! Keith? Is that you? I told you not to be here. What are you doing here?"

Theo did not pause. "You have a man who lives in your house?"

"No! No. He doesn't live here. He's renovating the bathroom. Seriously, he is the workman. Tell him Keith. Tell him you work for Ray."

"He doesn't look like he is working for Ray. He's sitting in your lounge room! In the dark!"

Keith blinked as the light was turned on. He seemed stunned, like a rabbit in headlights. A truant caught out of school grounds could not have looked guiltier. "Sandra told me you didn't have a man."

Theo stood up tall, his solid frame bulking out. "Well what do I look like? You can leave fully reassured that I am a man and she has me. You are obviously not fully abreast of the situation. You need to go."

31

"A breast…" he sniggered.

"Seriously? You are going beyond disrespecting. Creeping around in the dark spying on ladies. Do it again and I'll have you arrested you sicko!" Now Theo was truly infuriated.

Keith sort of scuttled to the door and was gone. It was quiet for a moment. I turned trembling back to Theo, and he poured me a drink as he stood there shaking his head. The charm of this little hut, with its basic rustic appeal had finally collapsed. Perhaps in daylight it might return. "You know. Would you mind if I took you up on your previous offer for tonight? This place may seem less unnerving in daylight… but just now… I don't care to stay. I'll pay for the room… you don't have to donate to the Tess fund."

"I'll drive you back early in the morning. No one need know you abandoned your plan."

"I don't care what other people think."

"Sure, you do. This is the whole point." And he opened the door and walked me to the car.

A voice from the shadows muttered. "You're going back with him? You really have a man?"

"Oh Keith, did you think we would be doing this if we didn't have feelings for each other? Come on. That would be just a little bit 'teenager' for us. I'm going back to his place, and I'm going to stay the night." Well… sort of. Subtle did not work with Keith. "Don't wait up. And don't be here when I get back." How many times, in how many blatant ways could a single message be said?

"It might not work out. I could come back…"

32

Theo stepped towards him. "Leave her alone! Or I will involve the police. Fixing the bathroom is your job – nothing more. Get it? This stops now. Are we clear?"

"But if you…"

"Skedaddle! Now!" and his tone was how he yelled at the stray dogs that poke around the garbage bins in the alley behind the pub.

I got in the car, and shivered. Together we had put on quite a performance. Theo drove in silence for a bit. "You okay?"

"Yeah, I am, thank you. The man's a creep. Persistent and deluded, I will give him that… but a creep none the less."

"Why didn't you mention it before?"

"Thought maybe I was over-reacting. I still kind of believe he is harmless enough. I had a friend who was in a domestic-violent relationship. She was seriously afraid he would kill her – it's not like that. I just thought Keith would dry up and give out. But it has intensified… and now I feel at any point he could tip over and get physical."

"Well, I'm glad you told me." We drove in silence for a while.

"Theo?"

"Hmm?"

"That kiss…"

"Don't mention it."

"But…"

"No seriously. Don't mention it." And the subject was closed.

6.

If I had been worried that my creativity might be drained by a casual job, I had not anticipated how this whole Keith thing might pull the plug on it. I was rattled. I'd walk around the cottage and the things that once inspired me, now reminded me of him skulking in the shadows. I'd sit at my computer and try to connect with Meg and her life. I went for a walk around the farm and sat looking at the trees and the dirt and the sheep and the kangaroos, but when I saw Keith at a distance walking over to his station-wagon, I went straight back home and locked the door. No writing that day either. I was angry that he had spoiled it for me. I was disappointed in myself that I just couldn't call it for what it was and get on with what I loved. The joy was gone. It was interfering with me on a pretty grand scale.

In desperation, I told Ray I'd be gone all week and took my laptop back to the pub. I looked at Theo apologetically as I walked in. He raised his eyebrows and nodded. Someone was eating a late breakfast in my corner, so I stuck my things behind the bar and just waited on tables for a while. I was grateful for a distraction. I got stuck into the monthly cleaning in the kitchen with a frenetic sort of focus. Ramon just let me be and continued at his grill. When the customers left my corner, Theo wiped down the table and stuck a reserved sign on it for me. Ramon came past while I was scrubbing skirting boards and handed me a schedule of jobs from his folder. "That's it Pet," he said, "Scrub it away; just for as long as you need." With unusual efficiency, I completed every listed task.

34

Late in the afternoon I sat with a coffee for a few minutes. Theo came over with another and sat down with me. "Feel better?"

"No, not really. I'm furious. He's spoilt it for me. What do I do now? Do I leave and try and find another place? I have waited so long to find the perfect writer's retreat, and this was it. But now it is contaminated by his perverted little visits and I am beginning to think there is no hope of retrieving how it used to be. I haven't written a word for weeks."

"Weeks? Serious."

"You're mocking me."

"No. Taking advantage of your frustration. Do you realise that this little fiction-writer just completed our entire monthly-clean in record time? Never seen this place shine with such intensity."

"Oh." He hadn't asked me to do any of this. I hadn't thought about that. "Will you pay me?"

"If you log the hours, I'll pay you." And he quickly left to attend to a regular patron.

Well. That wasn't as reassuring as it was perhaps intended to be. I didn't want to take advantage and log extra hours without approval. Perhaps that was what he was getting at. Still – he did promise to pay my hours. He had, since that unmentionable kiss, seemed more... distant. If my contentment had become restless, his 'easy-going' had turned business.

I noticed that if Theo wanted to know something he generally would ask straight out. Grab the bull by the horns and get the heart of the matter. I, on the other hand, prefer a sleuthing approach to clarifying situations that unsettled me. I look for clues; hints that would otherwise go unnoticed. These types of observations are breath to a writer. I drank my coffee slowly and tried to subtly disguise my intense scrutiny. Where Theo normally had a story or a funny anecdote to share with a customer, he now poured drinks or took orders without banter. Yes, I was right. Something was amiss. I had intended to go back to my computer after my coffee break, but I knew I would still be looking blankly at my screen. I was also avoiding going to the cottage, so as evening settled, I tackled another neglected cupboard in the alcove by the back door, and allowed myself to become absorbed in my thoughts as I sorted through accumulated crap.

Theo came into the kitchen and clipped up an order. I was a fly on the wall, observing unnoticed. His back was towards me as he picked up an olive on a toothpick and ate it. That was another sign of agitation. I had never witnessed him randomly taste-test the garnishes before. Ramon slapped his wrist and looked at him significantly and said, "That is not restless… I reckon it's nesting."

Theo spat the pip into the bin in disgust, "Damn business…"

Then Ramon moved closer. He cupped his hand under Theo's buttock in a most suggestive way and leaned in to whisper in his ear. Theo firmly removed his hand and chuckled. He sort of shook himself awake. "Perhaps you're right. Back to work then," he said as he returned to the bar.

I felt an electric shock run through me to the bone. I stumbled out the back trying to catch my breath in the warm evening air. Disorientated, I threw my apron on the wheelie bin and walked. I wasn't sure which direction I took, but I needed to move. I hadn't realised until then, I had pinned a great deal of hope on the idea that this friendship would not just stay friend-to-friend.

How naive was I really? In all the stories that I told, all the human narratives I have shared, I should have recognised that truth is never very far from the surface. That picture burned into my retina. He had told me those rumours about the cook were a constructed sort of world for a straight guy to have space. I was truly idiotic! I struggled to remember exactly how he said it, but it wasn't clear. Perhaps Theo had never actually said that at all. Perhaps I had suggested it to myself because I wanted it to be true. I had just joined the queue of people who made assumptions that were never corrected because it was convenient. I couldn't blame him for that. That was my doing.

I slowed my pace and took a deep breath. And another. Well it did actually make sense. He didn't want to talk about that kiss because it was a fabricated moment that wasn't real. It was a mistake from the outset, a discordant happening in his gay-world that needed to be buried. It was just part of his charade. It was only me who had made that kiss more than it was. I took another breath and looked around. I was in the park, blocks from the pub. Well. I could use the heartbreak as data for another story. Another life-experience that perhaps Meg or some other protagonist could benefit from.

I wondered then what he thought about me pouring out my confusion to him. All of the confessions I had offered in a transparent baring of myself. He might not know it, but he knew more of me than any other person on the planet. Tragic but true. Theo Delacey, the gay pub-owner, was my confidant.

I had believed he was my cherished soul-mate. I felt it was a special connection, but perhaps I wasn't unique. Perhaps what he said about 'confidant' was his generic contribution to the community at large. Nothing extraordinary. Nothing special. I had been so shy about it at first. Metaphorically, I'd test the water to see how he would respond to my private thoughts and feelings, like a seductive exposing of my shoulder now and then. But I became increasingly comfortable with stripping off my entire emotional garb until I was naked and sharing my most intimate thoughts without pause. I felt like a slut. I was so ashamed. Why had I not seen this coming. I think in that moment I understood what he meant when he had said 'sideswiped'. No. That didn't cover it: I felt steam-rolled.

I walked back to the car and drove home. If the hut seemed contaminated by the ongoing saga of the Keith episodes, then the pub just became radio-active. I walked in and Keith was cooking an omelette. I went straight over to the stove and threw the frying pan on the floor and turned off the gas. I swore and picked up the eggflip. "Get out of my house! Do you want me to call the police? Get out! Permission to renovate is hereby suspended. Get out! Get out!" I slapped him with the eggflip like swatting a pesky fly. And he flailed and flapped and backed away with pleas of taking him back. "Keith. I never left you. That was your wife. Your wife left you! You need to go to her. Cook an omelette for her. She is the one you miss. Go and sort it out with her. I am not that person!" And I shut the door and locked it on his devastated face. Not now. I couldn't deal with him now.

I sat there for I don't know how long. I curled up on the lounge and hid myself under a blanket and hoped that my humiliation would be covered by the shadows.

I stirred as I heard the knocking. I scrambled for my phone in the dark. It was after midnight. There were dozens of missed calls. I didn't move. I didn't want to see anyone. I didn't want anyone to see me. I couldn't risk it being Keith again. The vehicle drove away, and I knew of course it had been Theo.

The next day I sent a text message to say I wouldn't be coming in to work.

There was a quick question back: Was I okay? Did I need anything?

No thank you. Just not feeling well.

Mid-morning, I went and spoke to Ray. I told him that Keith had violated our agreement yet again and that I had decided to withdraw my cooperation with the renovation project. If that was unsuitable then we would both have to agree that I move out.

Ray told me Keith had packed up and left. He had woken up this morning muttering something about cooking Babette omelettes and they were wondering if he had had a complete breakdown. But then, in the next breath, Ray asked that if they managed to get another professional tradesman – not family, would I reconsider? Just Tuesday and Thursdays, to take the pressure off. I said I would think about it and let him know next week. I went home and lay on the lounge and cried. Keith

39

was gone but he had destroyed something very special to me in the process. In some way I was sure he was definitely responsible for Theo's orientation.

Late that night, there was another knock. I sat in the shadows immobilised. I felt like I had taken on Keith's bizarre dysfunctional coping. I heard the back door open and the laundry light came on. In the dim light reflecting through the open door I saw him framed there. Again, the pain of what I had learnt stabbed me in the chest. I had been so guarded. He was right: I didn't come looking for this. I wasn't on the prowl. And even when the idea became a possibility, I had not launched myself at him shamelessly. At least not to start with. He sought me out. Every encounter he was reeling me in with his smile and great coffee. Even if I had posed that question light-heartedly, I was checking the facts. And I had thought he had responded genuinely. Yet the reality was: I never was in for a chance. He had constructed this complicated scenario to keep me at bay. More believable I guess because of its convoluted trail. Hook, line, and sinker. His story had duped the storyteller. He had even asked me to trust him! And I had. What a nightmare! I was part of that inconvenient, intrusive world that he had needed to keep out.

His frame filled the doorway. "You okay? You left your computer under the bar. I was worried. I've never seen it out of your sight."

Would I reassure him I was fine? I was not. I wrote of heartache in my stories with an air of noble tragedy, but this hurt in a way that I was ignorant of. This was beyond gut-wrenching. "Oh. Yes. I forgot I left it. You didn't have to bring it out though. You can leave it on the table."

40

"You *forgot?* Okay... well, it's on the table."

"Thank you."

"Damn it, Tess. I'm turning the light on." The room filled with glare and I squeezed my eyes shut. He came over to me and stopped short. He swore. "What happened to you? Did Keith do this?"

I shook my head. It occurred to me that I must have looked truly horrendous to get such a reaction. Well, today 'frumpy' became a reality. I didn't care. What was the point of honest and transparent when love always slithered out of reach? I felt such venom building in my glands that I was sure that if I opened my mouth I would spit in his eyes. Part of me wanted to do that. To hurt like I was hurting. Somehow, I held my tongue. Forked tongue though.

He sat down on the coffee-table just across from me and waited. I was pretty sure I could out-wait him. And my mind yelled every accusation of his reprehensible behaviour and condemned my willing naivety to believe his lies. What would he care if I had misread every cup of coffee, every smile, every generous gesture, every quiet compliment, every shared joke... and that kiss? That kiss! How unfair was that kiss?

After a long while, he got up to leave. I sighed. Relieved. I knew I had survived, and I was feeling of a sort pious victory that I had managed to out last him. He would go because he had work to attend to tomorrow. He always had work tomorrow.

But he didn't leave. Instead he went to the kitchen and I saw him consider the omelette smeared on the floor with the frying pan left undisturbed where it had fell. He stepped over it and flicked on the jug. He made two cups of coffee. He paused a moment as he opened the fridge door. Then he quickly put milk in mine. He had his black and returned to his possie. He put my coffee within reach and drank his silently.

I felt like he was luring me out. After forty or so minutes I picked up my cup. It was cold. Obviously, it would be. He quietly took it from my hand and went and made two more fresh cups. This time he picked up the frying pan and put it in the basin and dumped the omelette in the bin. He efficiently wiped up some of the splatter with paper towel while the jug boiled. I sat up as he handed me the mug. I drank. I didn't even know exactly how I would tell him what this was about. He made a good coffee and a wave of grief resurfaced. I pushed it down as I swallowed. Time enough to cry when he was gone. I understood my grief then: he was gone. Sadness over my loss... even while he was alive and sitting in front of me. Although it had been one sided, never intended, it had been real to me. And now it had changed so completely.

I took a deep breath. I needed to go back to that adage, the one I had used over and over: friend-to-friend. Theo particularly had capacity to be a friend. I knew this. Perhaps his way of being was one of the reasons we had connected so perfectly. In the end, although this may be the problem, it may also be my way out; because, right now I desperately needed a friend. He had waited. That meant something.

That helped. I drank my coffee as slowly as I could, and made myself promise that when I got to the bottom of my mug, as a friend, I would try and explain the confusion as best I could. He probably knew anyway.

Finally, I took the last mouthful. I put the mug down and sighed. I pulled a tissue from the box. I looked at him and tears

42

welled. I squeezed them shut. Okay. I'm not going to look at him. I'll just say it. "Keith has left. He was here when I got home yesterday, cooking me the omelette and I lost it. I hit him with the egg-flip..."

"You're heart-broken because he's gone? I didn't expect that." He sounded shocked.

"No! Of course not! Should have done it weeks ago. Ray says he's gone for good."

"Oh. I thought you were saying you were in love with him."

"Huh." I shuddered. "Demonstrated by chasing him out of my house with the egg-flip. Creepy Keith's gone. *That* is a relief."

"I would have enjoyed watching that, if the placement of the frying pan is anything to go on."

I shook my head and smiled through my tears. It was like our way of being together... was being retraced. I wanted to pretend that nothing had changed. Except... I knew what I knew, and I could not ignore it. "I've told them I don't want the renovations to continue and that I will move out if that doesn't work for them. They are going to try and secure a different tradie if I'll reconsider. I said I would think about it." I stalled, and picked up my cup. It was empty. Of course.

"Want another?"

I nodded. Another margin to gather courage while he made two more cups.

He sat down again. "So, this is not about Keith leaving... but the Keith problem is essentially solved."

I nodded. "That's about it." I took a mouthful. I swallowed. "Theo, I know."

"Oh. You know." He nodded. "You know what?"

"That the rumour is not a rumour."

He frowned. Focused. "Rumour?"

"About you and Ramon being a couple. That's okay. It really is. It's just that I thought... I had hoped... that..." Tears filled my eyes again and I blew my nose.

"Oh. Well. That explains a lot."

"Explains what?"

"Why you ran out like a school-girl and haven't answered my calls, or the door. You called in sick, avoided coming to the pub... even when it involved the custody of your beloved computer."

"I was taken by surprise. I've been trying to get my head around it. I actually believed you. Which obviously..." I stopped and shrugged.

"Obviously... was what?"

"A mistake."

"Why?"

"Because you are."

"I am?"

"Well you would know."

"One would think so. You seem certain."

"I saw you together. You cannot deny it."

He scowled. "You saw us kiss? I don't think so. Never remember doing that."

"I know you have been careful, and very respectful of other people's reservations, but I don't know why you just couldn't tell me the truth without this charade about being straight pretending to be gay, which in the end is not pretending. It doesn't make sense."

44

"I would have to agree."

"See! What? You agree?"

"Well, it doesn't make sense at all, does it? Why would I do that? Why not just let the rumours tell their story and go with that? Far less complicated... and more effective if my goal was to keep you away."

"That's what I don't get. I was doing okay. You said I was content. I was! I had no intentions. And now... I find this out. I feel like I have lost a great deal, even when you never meant..."

"You forget something..."

"What am I forgetting?"

"That kiss."

"Oh, I have not forgotten that kiss! How could I? But I've realised that's why you won't talk about it... because it was just an act in the Keith's Benefit Performance. You do deserve an Oscar by the way."

He considered me for a long while. Eventually he said, "I didn't want to talk about it – not because it was a mistake, but because it was... beautiful. I didn't want to spoil that with banter. It was like a sacred moment for me. I wanted to keep it that way. Protect it."

"What..." I whispered. I frowned and closed my eyes. "It was real?"

"It was. Very real. For me at least..."

I paused. "So now I am confused... Oh no. Theo, I don't go in for bi-sexual relationships. I can't do that."

"Shouldn't be a problem then. I'm not big on sharing when it comes to relationships. In fact, I would expect us to be exclusive."

45

"You would?"

"Tess... if we did this... I would not be sharing you with anyone."

"So, you are saying that you and Ramon are not an item? That everything you told me was correct. You are straight. And single. And I am in for a chance?"

"As far as chances go, if I was a betting man, I would seriously back this one."

"But I saw you..."

"What did you see? Was his partner there? Blonde guy, good abs."

"No, it was you. In the kitchen. After my frenzied cleaning, I was running out of jobs, so I was clearing out the cupboard near the back door. You came in really agitated, and you were picking at the food. Ramon slapped your fingers and he said something that really annoyed you. Then he came over and held your butt. He whispered in your ear. It was very intimate... and not at all straight, I assure you. You didn't push him away. You just muttered something and went back to work."

"I have told you Ramon is gay, right? That explains it."

"Not really."

He drained his cup and seemed like he wasn't sure what else to say. "Okay... well yes, I was agitated. I was... am. You were talking about leaving. I didn't know what to do about that. Ramon knows how I feel. He was trying to reassure me that you weren't going. He thought that all the cleaning was actually a sign that you were preparing to settle in... he said it was "nesting". It didn't seem possible, but I was hoping he was right. Yeah, he touched my butt. He does that sometimes. It's not something I encourage, and it probably feeds the rumours. Then he said to me… what he said." He stopped and shrugged.

"You're not going to tell me?"

"It was kind of… a bit inappropriate."

I frowned. "I would like to know what he said."

He paused and swallowed. "Seriously?"

I nodded.

"Okay. He said…" He stopped and swallowed.

"Well?"

"You really want to know?"

I nodded again with raised eyebrows.

"Okay. He said, *'Don't worry Theo, that nice little tush of yours will soon get the action it deserves'*."

I laughed out of relief. He had no idea how that absurd little comment was music to my heart. "Well it's probably not the most offensive thing that your pub walls have ever heard."

"I wasn't offended by it at all. It actually gave me courage; until I came looking for you and you were gone. I retrieved your apron from off the wheelie-bin. Then I found your computer still there and your car gone. It felt like that summer-from-hell all over again. I didn't know what had happened. I haven't moved the reserved sign in your corner. I thought about putting candles and flowers there as a shrine."

I shook my head. "You are being very melodramatic. Are you sure you're not gay?"

"That's not the half of it. I rang up an agent about selling the pub. If you weren't coming back, I was going. I still might if you won't do this, because I am pretty sure I can't… getting too old to go through this again."

47

My eyes stayed glued to his face; every line etching permanently into my mind. "Do you want something to eat? I haven't eaten for at least a day."

"You have omelette."

"I suppose I could retrieve that... and add salmonella sauce. Could make a fresh one. Or French toast with bacon."

"Let's go with toast and bacon."

I went to the fridge and opened the door. Then he was there, and he gently removed the carton of eggs from my hand and put them on the bench. He cradled his hand in the small of my back and ran his other hand behind my neck. He kissed me... slowly, boldly, passionately. And there was strength in knowing there was not a shred of play-acting involved.

7.

It was like a dam wall had burst open: floods of sharing and crying and laughing and loving and talking. I had never been one to do things by halves. When I wanted to write a story, then I quit my job, and left town to immerse myself in it. I wondered how this newfound dimension to our relationship would interfere with my plan. I was sure it would, but I guess I wondered by how much, and if in the end, whether that even mattered anymore.

Was it really a problem if I lost Meg and Ben's story, now that I had my own story to savour and hold? But my story was not one I wanted to share with the world. This was my own private romance... being believed and loved by someone who saw me, who made an effort to understand me, embrace me... the frumpy bits and the ugly bits... without the DIY dieting advice; or trying to change my dress code; or fix the way I stand; or better my mind by telling me what books I ought to read; or make me into some picture that they thought I should be. That was what I loved about Theo: his whole-hearted, unapologetic acceptance.

In the past I wondered if my obsession with my blended historical-fictional character-friends was a vicarious take on the life I never got to live. Now that would be tested. I had Theo, so did that mean my literary friends would disappear and fade and I'd never see their faces again? I wondered if I might grieve their going, or whether their romance might lie dormant on some cyberspace-drive, with their tale untold. Would they seek out their revenge on me for abandoning them? I felt like some malevolent Roman Caesar, who went to his family one evening, kissed them good-night and then murdered them in their beds. Someone who had been their creator and protector, was now the instrument of their betrayal and death.

Theo had left late, and I lay that night on my pillow, listening to a noisy cricket in the corner of the bathroom chirrup away with incessant persistence. I tried to close my eyes and my ears, but it was a frequency that refused to be ignored. I rolled over and resigned myself to wakefulness and wondered what my story-friends might do with that cricket. Ben got up and found it and took it outside with a dry explanation that he wasn't going to kill it for calling for his mate. Meg took her boot and stomped on it because that was the quickest solution to getting sleep. Everett demanded his poorly paid house servant make it go away. He didn't care how.

As I lay there seeing each of them deal with this annoying little creature, I realised something quite remarkable. They weren't fading. They weren't disappearing into a mist in cyberspace, but they were as tangible and reactionary and as real to me as ever. More so. And it was like they were demanding that I get up and write, like that insistent little cricket. Though I was tired, I knew I would not sleep unless I submitted, at least for a little while, to the process of clicking away at the keyboard. I had no way of knowing; no way of pre-empting what their future would be like now that my arms were occupied with a love of my own. I got up and made myself a cup of tea. I retreated into Meg's hut and continued to write.

Healthy, honest, transparent conversation had lifted Keith's contamination in the little stone cottage, and it felt wholesome again. I avoided all other people. The days I worked at the hotel, I couldn't wait to get home and visit with them: find out what they were doing; where they were; how they were rising to their challenges; how they were getting up again if they fell over. If Earnest Hemmingway had said, *'There is nothing to writing at all – you just sit at the typewriter and bleed'*, it wasn't that way for me. It was like my airways were cleaned, and my antenna were tuned; and I could hear... and see... and feel... with greater clarity. Health, not haemorrhaging, sanctioned my creative sight. Obviously, my work was not Hemmingway either, but I didn't care. My friends were safe. Their story could continue to be told.

After Theo turned off the main lights and closed the front doors, I walked over to him. I draped my arms around his neck. "Thank you. I have written so much in the last three weeks. It's flowing like I have never seen. It is amazing for me!"

He sighed and carefully undraped my hands so he could push down the bolts to the floor. "Drought to a flood. That's very Australian."

'Yeah. Perhaps it is a bit like the weather. I don't feel I have control over it... but I just have to catch it when it runs. I suspect that you are mostly responsible for this glorious creative surge."

"Me? I don't feel like a weather-god. I just feel neglected."

"Neglected? Really? Is this bad?"

"Neglect is never my plan. I like your attention. We haven't had any time at all this week. Or last week actually."

"Oh Theo, I'm sorry. I've just been so excited to get back into it. I wondered whether it was over, and I wouldn't see them again at all. I thought maybe I might not need them anymore. I wondered if writing is just for weak-willed people who don't have real relationships. It has been a relief, in a way, knowing that the story is still there."

"So... we're a 'real relationship'?"

"Yeah. Of course." I paused. He had obviously been thinking about this. Not in a petulant, woe-is-me sort of way. Just missing me, I guess. "What can I do to reassure you my neglect is not permanent?"

"Well I do appreciate that you acknowledge I have been neglected. And as it happens, I have a solution."

"Oh?"

"Give up writing and marry me."

"Don't be ridiculous. I'm serious. What can I do?"

"I am serious. Well, maybe not about giving up writing... but definitely the other part. Tess, will you marry me?"

I was standing there in the dark, the smell of pub around me, the front of his apron a little grimy and he was proposing to me. Not the stuff of novels. But in the most organic, unpretentious, genuine sort of way, it was. My story.

We kissed. "Is now a good time to point out we have only officially been going out for three weeks, most of which you accuse me of neglect? Does this seem kind of premature to you?"

"No. You've been my exclusive study since I laid eyes on you. I have no doubt."

"Well, obviously I can't know you all that well. Three weeks ago, I would have backed a truckload you were gay."

"You really are not going to let that go, are you? Do I have to sack Ramon?"

"Wow. Now I feel important. The sacrifices you are willing to make. No of course you can't sack Ramon! You need him and his food. I just feel like it is... well, you know... kind of quick."

"Quick? Oh, you are a funny one. I've been waiting for you forever."

"Romantic notion, but really... three weeks?"

"So, you are not sure?"

"Well, yesss..."

"So, what's the problem?"

"What are people going to think about you dumping the cook for a barmaid?"

"They can think what they like. They have up to now. I know you have been on their radar for a while now. They know something is going on. I would just like to clear up exactly what."

"By marrying me."

"Uh huh."

"Theo, when I first came and sat in your corner... you used to tell them something... about who I was and what I was doing, and they'd leave me alone. What were you telling them?"

"That you were a cleaver wielding escapee from a mental institution who would track them down and murder them in their bathrooms."

"Come on. Really – what did you tell them?"

"Hmm. I went with a freelance writer for a travel site – we were never really sure which one. You were doing a series of reviews on local country pubs."

"Freelance critic? Part fact, part fiction. Clever."

"Reviewers are a mysterious bunch: feared and hated and respected… and consequently everyone here has been checking every travel and dining site on the web with religious fervour ever since. They've added their ratings to counter whatever poor appraisal you were going to give. Ratings have gone up… significantly."

"Where's their faith? I might have written a good review."

He laughed. "That's what I said, but they were not willing to leave it to you or to chance. And they were speculating on which particular reviews were yours. I think Mick may have had a book on that at some stage as well. They were all a little possessive and very defensive. You did not look happy much of the time."

"What happened to content?"

"I think it was mostly a combination of Keith and whatever was happening in your story at the time, but when that scowl was up, every phone and tablet within cooee came out. I would feed you complimentary stuff and then everyone would wait to see what you did. If I told them that you thought it was better than the last pub, then they would have to try it… again, just to check. I got heaps of good orders."

"I tell you… you should go in for story-telling yourself. I can't believe you sold them that I had the credible look of an undercover food-critic."

"But when you spoke with that Italian couple… that nailed it. The way you prattled on in Italian and did the wine tasting thing. All very impressive."

I laughed. How simply something could change into what it was not at all.

"But it gets better. Ramon wanted to change his menu, so I took you the deleted item; I told you an off story so you would scowl or splutter your food. I told them you called it something really quite offensive and that's why we were taking it off the menu. Mostly they agreed no one liked it anyway. It was good fun."

"I think I deserve a retainer as a Change Management strategy: new menu, no complaints, all good reviews? That's got to be worth something. You have innovative strategies if nothing else!"

"Innovative. Strategic. Yep. That's me."

"Ahh... those random comments about this heritage pub being good enough to stay at and work in. That is all making so much more sense..." I had merely agreed with locally grown loyalty and was more than once bemused by the fervent waves of approval I received.

"And I haven't forgotten my original question, which I think you are avoiding."

"Okay. I'll marry you... but let's wait a while before we tell anyone. Just between us?"

"I've got to keep this under my hat? Why? How long is a while?"

"I like the idea that I have this private world, that no one else sees. It feels so intimate... contained... special. I want you, and this, to myself for a while. Protect it... from banter. Without sharing..."

"I have no reply. I cannot think of one possible argument that suitably responds to my own incredible wisdom. It makes me want to keep our secret forever. Is this what it is like to have an affair?"

I frowned at that. And swallowed. "I wouldn't know. We'll see how your story-telling holds up under pressure."

"No problem. No problem at all."

8.

I settled back into my corner. I was increasingly enamoured with the idea of a functioning bathroom and laundry sooner rather than later, so I offered Ray the whole working week so the new tradesmen could get in and finish the job. For the amount of time Keith spent there, I'm not sure how much work he actually accomplished. There were the usual renovation problems of installing in an old place, and I was glad it was not my headache to manage. Besides... it was not hard to sit in Theo's corner.

I became so distracted, my newly found literary flow had stemmed to a mere trickle. I started washing windows just to get myself out of the habit of daydreaming inappropriately. I sat down after the midday rush and waited for Theo to bring his coffee and lunch over. He didn't. He went up to the post-office and ran a dozen errands in an uncharacteristic frenzy of efficiency. Ramon made cute comments about his little lovebirds pretending to fly off in different directions. I made myself a fresh coffee and sat looking at my manuscript with a kind of dazed disappointment. I hadn't expected to react like this petulant child.

My characters confidently demonstrated over and over that there was more to them than what I initially saw. I didn't doubt the truth of this observation, but I wondered to what the extent I could delve into those under-currents. Right now, I did not know what was underneath or behind the characters sitting in front of me. Meg and Ben had found each other, but I couldn't leave the story there. This is where the stories usually ended, but this was not over. There were still things to learn about each other and I had hoped that because they were working things through, it was a reflection that my relationship with Theo was progressing positively as well. But nothing felt right at the moment; nothing was settled or resolved.

I resented Theo's inattention with a jealous intensity that shocked me. The late lunch ritual was our time. At least I had thought it was. When he got back, he was in fine form. The anecdotes were flowing; the jokes and quips were sharp. His smile was amiable. Easy-going was back. He focused in on his female customers with carefree attention, and ignored me with careful intention. It lasted all week. On Friday one of the men made a comment and Theo called out to me. "Tess, Ted here says the men's room needs attention. Could you fix that please?"

I was stunned. It was the first time Theo had ever spoken to me like... well, like staff. I looked up from the computer where I had been surfing useless websites fact-checking the history of the Australian police-force and cattle duffing and shut the lid to my computer just a little too firmly. Unbelievable! I checked the clock and went out the back and grabbed the bucket and mop. I was in the middle of mopping furiously with more steam coming from under my collar than the hot water, when someone came in. "I'll be done in a tick. Use the disabled toilet if you don't mind." I had put up the signs. Why can't people read?

I turned as I heard the door lock. Theo took the mop from my hand. He didn't say anything, putting it back in the bucket. Then he kissed me, and I melted. "You're not liking this secret thing, are you? Do you want to continue? Can I go public?"

"This is blackmail.   I wasn't counting on a shunning. You haven't had lunch with me all week."

"I have not had lunch with anyone for years. If I continue with lunch... it's going to send a very strong message you are in my sights. I'm not going to eat by myself while you're sitting just there, so I go out or work in the office. This could be good for catching up on a backlog of admin."

"You are ignoring me deliberately..."

"I thought that was the plan."

"You spoke to me... like a serf!"

"If you're not my girl-friend, you are staff."

"Damn you are good."

"Glad you appreciate that. After I close up... can we talk, hang out, make out, have a date?"

"Sure. I'll hang around..."

I finished mopping and emptied the bins. I really doubted that I could do this. All week I was living with the revelation that 'secret' was not as romantic as I thought it would be. Why not go public? What was my hesitation? Was I ashamed? Of him... or me... or us?

I coveted Theo's attention so deeply, and I was not ashamed of our relationship. I cherished it. So, what was going on with me? I finally settled on the time-frame. It was too soon. I wanted this little rural community of loyal devotees to be convinced I was not a fly-by-nighter. If their faithful rallying generated five-star ratings on their travel logs, they would not stand by and see their Theo dive into a dubious relationship with a nobody from goodness-knows-where. As I waited that evening for Theo to close up, I continued to mull over this dreadful dilemma.

When he finally turned out the lights it was a relief, we could be ourselves. "So... I have been thinking about what you said this afternoon."

He grinned. "I told you I'd have no trouble with your challenge. You missed me! One week... that's all it took." And I imagined he was formulating announcements to be plastered all over: banners hung from balcony-rails, flyers stapled to streetlight posts; community blogs and social media boards. He looked kind of smug and I allowed him to enjoy his moment of victory. Briefly.

"Yes... but don't get too excited. I want to propose something."

"Marriage? I accept." He kissed me with a hint of amusement and then pulled back. "Of course, not – marriage would be too simple. My little fiction-writer has a head for intrigue."

"The thing is..." and I described my unease. His loyal friends and patrons would not stand by and watch him get his heart broken again... particularly by an outsider.

"I think you over estimate their care-factor. Or is it that you think I can't win your heart on my own?"

"Well obviously you have. But whether you want to admit it or not, they do care. They need to be in on it... or they could start giving ratings that are completely against me... and the whole thing could go bust."

"You really believe that our relationship stands and falls on their say so? Well, I don't think so."

"Theo?"

"Hmm?"

"I am not the only one who loves you. They will not let you do this if they are not convinced, I am good for you. You have to let them help problem solve this with you."

"Why? There's no problem."

"You also have to protect Ramon. That could be tricky if they have really bought in on the cook-thing; a thing you have allowed to persist... even encouraged."

"You've thought about this all day, haven't you?"

"No. It's been bugging me all week."

"Okay. If you..."

"I do..."

He grinned. "I like the sound of that."

"Huh. Really?"

"Going to trust me on this then?"

"Completely," I said confidently.

"Promise me you'll come in every day next week?"

"Of course. There is still only part of a bathroom at home, and I do need a flushing loo."

I thought that it might be sweet to set the scene for his overtures of fondness to begin, if I went back to those initial comfortable jeans and coffee moments. But as soon as I walked through the door on Monday morning in my favourite denims, it felt like I had stepped off the Star Ship Enterprise and landed on an alien planet. Theo growled irritably at everyone, like he was living with a perpetual hangover. Ramon rolled his eyes and said, "What's got into him? That boy is like a giant blackhead that I just want to squeeze." I couldn't agree with him more!

"Are you going to do any work today?" Theo snapped at me. There were only a few patrons around, but he had never, ever aired his grievances in public like that before! I got snippy right back at him.

"I told you they're renovating all this week. We agreed I would do my usual hours on Tuesdays and Thursdays. Today is Monday. Not working."

"Well it would nice to have someone who would offer some help when they can see there are things to do."

"Well if it bothers you so much I'll sit outside, so you don't have to look at me sitting here, lolling about!" I was planning on writing and I was not intending on changing my plans.

"Fine!"

I gathered my computer and walked outside and sat at one of the courtyard tables near a window. I could still see him at the bar, swinging around like an agitated primate. He grabbed a glass and it smashed in his grip, cutting the palm of his hand. He picked out the glass fragments in disgust and wrapped it with a tea towel. One of his regulars named Joanie, rang the doctor, and drove him to the surgery. He came back with stiches and a bandaged hand. He was still banging and clanging things around inside.

Oh boy. I hadn't realised how angry he was about this. Now he was going to make sure the plan went belly-up to expose its stupidity. I pulled out a tissue and wondered why I didn't just do things without this compulsive need for control. It was all so screwed up. But in a way I was thankful I was seeing this side of him. I was right to hesitate. I saw that now.

Joanie came out and sat down at my table with her drink.

"So? Do you like him or not?"

That was kind of straight to the point. I hedged. "I thought he was gay." Well. I actually had thought that… at one point.

"Theo? Gay? I don't think so. He is as gay as Ramon is straight."

"Oh. Are you sure? I'd heard stuff…"

"Oh yes. I'm sure. But I would know, because, well, we used to… have a thing."

I put my hand up and shook my head. "I don't need to know. Really!"

So, Joanie delightedly launched into explaining how Theo had hurt his hand accidently, but she suspected it was actually accidently-on-purpose, because he wanted me to come inside and work some extra hours.

"Seriously? He is being incredibly rude! He can show some decency and come and ask me himself." What was with the messenger girl?

"So, you don't like him then."

"Liking a person doesn't mean they can treat you like something the cat dragged in."

"So, you do like him?"

"I'd like an apology."

Joanie cringed. "Hmm, see… Delaceys are not apology sort of people. But Theo needs help in there, and he said his other casuals are not available just now."

"Well, that's the price of desperate. He comes in person and asks in person, or I don't go in."

Joanie sighed, and went back in to deliver the message. I glanced through the window and saw him raise his arms above his head in exasperation, pacing around behind the bar. If my pride hadn't been smarting so intensely it would have been quite an entertaining performance. I went back to my writing and tried to ignore their focused devotion. Heads were leaning forward. Advice was flowing. Eventually he downed a shot and made his way to the door and sat down at my table.

"I'm going to sit for a few minutes, and you can look either sad or irritated. Then please… please come in and help. This stings like hell and I have to keep it dry."

"Theo, please tell me you didn't do this deliberately! Are you nuts? If it's not an accident – they call that self-harming! What's got into you?"

"You didn't want to go public. This is me keeping it under wraps."

"Grief! This is insane."

"I'll actually confess I think this is a clever idea. They are coming on board. They will soon start to realise I'm madly in love…"

"I think they are going to realise you are plainly insane! You will get committed if you keep this up."

"And demanding I apologise… that is genius."

"I am actually serious. You can't treat me like pond-scum. That is not okay."

"Nah. Don't worry about it. It's great acting."

"This is the execution of your plan? Being obnoxious?"

"It was your plan, if memory serves me right."

"Oh, my goodness, you are properly scary. It is so real it is almost Keith all over again. How is that even possible? I never said anything about being detestable." I wiped my eyes and sighed. His logic somehow seemed flawed. At least he had come in person. He had met the brief. "Alright, I'll come in." I put my stuff under the bar and went to work.

I noticed that after the fictitious food-critic thing was laid to rest and it was obvious that my freelance-writing job was over, I developed a level of invisibility. As a casual pub-employee no one saw me; no one noticed who served their beer, as long as it was cold. No one cared whether I was in my corner or not. That suited me. But now that Theo had apparently disclosed being confused about his feelings for me, all of a sudden, I was visible again. Very visible. They scrutinised my work and deemed it relatively satisfactory. They raised their brows when they saw I wasn't going to be pushed around by Theo's tantrums. They discussed why Theo, who wasn't an apologising sort, had apologised to me. And when they found out that there actually had been other staff available and yet he insisted on me… that got them talking even more. How very odd and unaccountable. Theo was having some sort of crisis. Joanie's explanation became the circulating theory. Because his hand had to be kept dry that was reason enough for me to show for extra shifts, and I did work every day that week. I tried to find jobs that were in the kitchen or out of the way, so I didn't have to listen to them talk about Theo and his problems… or his belligerent directions at every turn.

By the end of the week, I was exhausted. Full time work did not suit me. The emotional energy required to survive the jibes and the attention was driving me to distraction. Friday afternoon, I abandon my work post and sat down at my table with my computer, and more than anything I just wanted to go visiting with Meg and Ben... and their rather undramatic lives. Maybe not good literature... but I just wanted out. I called their farm Petrea Downs... which is the feminine of Peter... "Rock". It was after all inspired by the Rocky Creek Farm B&B. And it did seem worthy to offer a reference to the old quarry on the property. It felt more like a reference to the rocky nature of my relationships. Still, that Rock was my retreat, my safe-place. I needed a virtual-visit.

Theo brought over a coffee. I barely noticed, but it had some of the same familiar rhythms we used to have. I glanced up and he hadn't moved. He was still standing, and it didn't look like he intended to sit. I shrugged, "What?"

"I thought you might say thank you."

I glanced around the room and every pair of eyes were on us. "Thank you?" I said tentatively. "What's going on?"

"I've been given a dare..."

"Good for you. Thank you for the coffee." And I went back to my story.

He grabbed me by my wrist and pulled me to my feet. He kissed me roughly on the mouth to a general sprinkling of applause. He paused, looking very smug, and without thinking I slapped him hard across the face. His eyes went from pleased to stunned. "What was that for?"

"Have a guess. You have never been so presumptuous and disrespectful. I am seriously... genuinely... not happy!"

There was no way I wanted him to think this was some sort of play-acting finale deserving curtain-call credits. I grabbed my computer and power cords and left. Greif. This had got so out of control.

9.

My grand plan hardly seemed to have a skerrick of sensible in it at all. I sat on my sofa at home and tried to work out where this had all gone wrong. Theo had asked me to marry him, and in a week, it had gone belly up. I trusted him just like he asked. Implicitly. But now I wasn't sure if he was putting on this act, or whether there was some sort of suppressed sociopath that was being unleashed. If this plan to get his community of pub-dwellers on-side had worked, now I was effectively off-side. Totally. I was utterly put-off by his week of unbridled misogynistic, uncouth, unapologetic male chauvinism. Where had my Theo gone? I missed *him*.

And then I wondered: what if I had just kissed him back? What if I had just let it slide? Pretty sure there would have been a cheer and a round of beers and Theo could have gone public. Simple. Why wouldn't I just let it be simple?

I got up and checked the progress on the bathroom tiling. It was all but done. Soon it would be finished. One less disruption. I could finally find some rhythm again. I thought I would make myself a salad. I stood at the fridge with the door open and tried to gather my thoughts. I imagined Theo there. Kissing me gently, inviting me to draw close. Not this disrespectful bravado that was akin to some brazen 19th century French stage-show. Nope, that was too classy: more accurately… the antics of a Neanderthal cave dweller.

I didn't feel hungry and closed the door. I made myself a camomile tea instead. I didn't know what to do. I had clouted him. Could I even pretend that didn't happen? Could I judge his theatrics, when my behaviour was like a black and white slapstick Laurel and Hardy movie? Comedy or... tragedy? Nothing funny about this. I couldn't decide which was worse. I felt the shame of it acutely.

I checked my phone. No messages. I went to send one... and then deleted every character... three times. I paced and then put on an exercise routine and pushed myself not to think about it. I still couldn't use the bathroom to have a shower, so washed up in a basin in my living room. I had just put on some house clothes when there was a knock at the door. I opened it. Theo was there. I stepped aside without saying anything.

"Tess... I..." He just stood there.

"I don't know what went wrong. I have no idea!" I was genuinely bewildered by the whole week. Tears stung my eyes.

"Well I..."

"I hit you! I am so sorry! Where did that come from? I didn't even hit my dog when I was training it. And yet I hit the man I am supposed to marry? That does not make sense! I feel so ashamed." I looked at him through my tears. "I am so sorry Theo. Please forgive me." He came over, but it was like he was not even sure if he was allowed to touch me anymore. I reached out and he met me almost with relief. "I'm sorry..." I repeated, and he hushed my words and gently kissed my forehead. This was the gentleman I was familiar with and reached up and kissed him.

"I was going to make a salad... do you want something to eat?" I could bet he had not eaten either. He nodded. It seemed food was our together language. We sat down, munching on a toss of lettuce and salad-veges with balsamic dressing. I looked across at him. "I think I was looking forward to being courted and seduced again. And I was shocked that instead you turned into this fireball of manic disrespect. I didn't know who that was." He looked as if it was a genuine revelation that I wasn't amused by the whole debacle. "And that kiss!" I shuddered.

Theo shook his head. "I thought you'd appreciate the dramatic being-swept-off-your-feet scene. You're making much more of it than it really was."

"Really! You were going for 'swept-off-my-feet'? Do you want to know what it was like? Sex without foreplay... or consent. I think they call that rape."

Theo put down his fork. "Hold on. I don't appreciate that!"

"Well where is the line? You treat me like a common maid. Does that come with conjugal privileges as well? What were you thinking?"

"I assure you I feel more like a monk than your boyfriend!"

"This was a mistake from the beginning."

"Perhaps it was!" He stood up abruptly and stared me down. Daring me to tell me he was wrong.

But I couldn't. More like... I wouldn't. He just didn't get what I was saying and what it meant to me. I had never felt so cheap. This whole idea was supposed to bring us together, instead I felt I had been paraded around the town square before the citizens in a shame parade. I did nothing to deserve that!

So, this was it. This was my break-up moment. It was not aggressive. No thrown kitchen knives. Just a realisation that this was going nowhere. I grimaced and shrugged. If I had a ring, I would have taken it off and handed it over. I almost wished I had that symbol to declare its finality. But I didn't and the moment sort hung suspended for a while. In the end, the silence became too loud, and he picked up his keys and walked out.

I sat down in the shadows and gave myself permission to cry. Something within me relished the pain, as if in some way it made me feel alive and real and not exempt from all the tragedy that I put my characters through. And then I realised that in our conversation since Theo arrived, I was sorry and I apologised, and he had just justified his arrogance. Telling.

On Monday morning I got a text message from Theo requesting that I come into the office and sort some employee paperwork. It sounded like he was sacking me, or maybe hoping I would just leave. It was very inconvenient that the money from this job was helpful. I was thinking about whether I could go him for unfair dismissal, or if my budget could afford my own melodramatic scene where I could tell him to shove his job.

I sent a text back. Couldn't it wait until tomorrow when I was in?

Not really. The accountant was on his back about it.

I walked in and there was a generous bouquet of flowers on my table in the corner with a card. I noticed them but said nothing. I wasn't going to presume they were for me. How embarrassing if they were not. I looked at Theo. "The forms are in here," he said officially, and he ushered me into his office.

He closed the door. He handed me a tax dec' form and a pen. I shrugged. "I've done one of those." I put them down.

"Tess, I got carried away. Tell me how to fix this."

71

"You want to fix it?" The silence of the weekend had been as loud as the whole week had been insufferable. I wondered if he considered I was like some leaky tap that needed a new washer and then everything would be just fine.

"Of course. We are good together. I want us back."

"Do you know what I want? I want us to treat each other with respect."

"Isn't this respectful?"

"But not just in private… what about when other people see us? Your behaving like Jekyll and Hyde."

"You want to keep it secret; then it's keep-them-in-the-loop. I'm wondering who is Hyde in this scenario?"

"I didn't just pull this out of a hat. We talked about this… we had a plan."

"The plan was to go public."

"This has nothing to do with that."

"Of course, it does. They are blaming themselves because they put up the dare."

"Theo, take some responsibility! This is not about them."

He looked at me like my antennae were showing and he suddenly realised I was an alien. I sighed. Nope. Not getting it.

"You seriously are putting this all on me? Oh, come on. You're behaving like I had an affair." He looked so frustrated. "You're the one who wanted to read them in. I was trying to accommodate your sense of the dramatic."

"Really? Dramatic? Like that is a good thing? You're trying to make it sound artistic, but nothing is a licence for insolence. Ramon called you a giant blackhead that he wanted to squeeze! As a metaphor I thought it was incredibly gross and exceptionally accurate."

He sat down on his office chair and sort of spun around like a lost little boy. I softened. "Given Ramon's skin care regime is something akin to a catwalk model, it was, at the very least, an observation that something was amiss," I said. I wasn't just going to say it didn't matter. It mattered.

He swore as if he suddenly realised something quite unexpected. He grimaced. "Tell me what I've got to do…" He had resigned himself to great exploits of contrition to demonstrate his sincerity.

"Really? You think this is fixable with a sad face and a little more play acting?"

"You know I'll do what I can to make it right. A thousand notes of apology. A hundred red roses on your pillow. Whatever it takes. I mean it Tess. This is worth fighting for."

"That's the thing: I don't want to fight. Had enough of that as a kid."

"Oh."

"I want respectful, caring, honest. They are my non-negotiables."

With reassurances we would talk more after work, I walked out of the office with the surreal feeling I was on reality TV. An unusual number of patrons were quietly sipping drinks, and they all turned in their seats in synchronised choreography. Of course, Joanie was there. As she quickly sat on her stool it had the sense that she was occupying the director's chair, guiding all proceedings moment by moment with artistic command. Yes, the flowers were for me. I smelt them and quietly shed a tear as I read the card. I saw out of the corner of my eye that the audience was waiting, expectant, fully anticipating more… so I took a deep shuddering breath, and tried to look as if I was making every effort to hold it together. I took drama as a subject at school too.

Theo managed to organise someone else to close-up and came out to the hut early enough to eat dinner. "Been thinking about this non-negotiable of yours. I understand now that it is a big-deal for you. Well, I can do big." His shoulders were relaxed like he had a plan. I was fast losing confidence in his plans.

"That's not want I meant. I just want real."

"Look. I guess in Ramon's world, we are 'out of the closet' now. Tess, let me try again: another week. I'll do it right. A public apology, for the public insult."

"I don't need any of this to be over-the-top. What happened to my laid-back and amiable Theo?"

"Why would you want laid-back and ordinary, when your life is all about larger-than-life story-telling? I want to be the guy who sweeps you off your feet; the one you get to fight with, so we can make up together."

"Theo, amiable is not ordinary. And you don't have to compete with my stories. I don't want my life like that. There will be enough opportunities for us to disagree. I don't think we have to generate them." I thought of the enormous bunch of flowers sitting in my corner booth. "Suddenly I'm terrified you're going to put up mirror balls and use smoke machines with a trail of cleansing flower petals on the carpet."

He looked confused. "Mirror balls aren't acceptable? Doesn't everyone get smoke machines with their public apologies?"

"Very funny. Tone it down. Okay? Sincere and normal. Can you do normal?"

"What about gifts? Please don't tell me it has to be poetry... because I will definitely need to plagiarise."

"I love gifts... normal gifts. No poetry. No giant teddy bears."

"Damn. That was Wednesday's gift of contrition."

"Choose something else. No... not negligée. Something suitable for public viewing."

"Wow. The parameters are coming thick and fast now."

"Just be you. I love the normal you. No raging monsters, slashing up their hands."

"So, you promise to come in every day this week?"

"Last time I promised that, it didn't end well. But I'm not writing much anyway... so okay, I'll be there."

"Huh. So, I've gone from weather-god to clogged sewer."

"I appreciate that you are taking responsibility for the blocked creativity." I didn't follow that metaphor further to where the fruits of my creativity were the stuff of septic tanks.

"Very well," I conceded. "Let's see what you can do with a week." And under the light of a three-quarter moon shining over the paddocks, we called a truce and discovered what it was like to make up.

Tuesday's surprise was an enormous box of beautiful Belgium chocolates. By the time I passed them around, I got to enjoy only one.

Wednesday. There was no giant teddy bear, which was a relief. There was a cheese plater laden with fresh fruit including imported fresh dates, and corny limerick about going on a date. His offering of poetry made me smile. At dinner-time Ramon appeared with candles and tablecloth, and a special menu with all my favourites. Theo had engaged one of the school kids to play his violin. After the second screeching tortured-cat song, I smiled and congratulated him on his playing. Theo gave him another tip before he left. I had insisted on normal but now I was wondering who defines what is typical, ordinary, normal, standard anyway?

Thursday. I figured Theo would have run out of ideas for normal and was dreading a little bit what he would come up with, but there was an envelope with two tickets to the town movie-night. In lieu of a movie theatre they were screening at the Town Hall. We ate popcorn and drank frozen coke. This normal was wonderful. At one point he put his arm around me and leaned over and pointed out at least three couples whom he understood had never gone to these nights since they began screening. They were sitting four rows back, immersed in their phones and hardly looked at the screen right up until the credits.

Friday. That was a surprise. There was nothing at the table except the flowers that were starting to wilt. I changed the water, pulled out the dying stems and trimmed off some of the rather limp flower heads. They looked a little fresher.

We had coffee together for morning-tea and we chatted amiably, even laughed a bit, to the satisfaction of everyone watching. I really couldn't get used to this idea of being constantly scrutinised. Theo shrugged. He said it was just small-town paparazzi, the scrutiny being a little heightened because of our dramatic spat last week. They didn't feel the need to pretend they were being covert anymore, because everyone knew something was going down, and it was their right to know as soon as it did. Theo brought a couple of ice-creams to go with our coffee, because he said I had given away the very best chocolates he could find in town on short notice on Tuesday. He also wanted an update on how he was going, and a rating out of ten for each of his gifts of contrition. I had to concede he had done exceptionally well.

It was then that he produced the pocket-sized gift box. I looked at him and smiled. Okay. This was perfect. I could hear the twittering in the background. I almost expected the bended knee, and I allowed myself to blush as I opened the box.

It was a necklace.

Oh.

Granted – it was a stunning diamond pendant with matching earrings… in a ring sized box. I actually felt disappointed, as beautiful as they were. And it occurred to me then, that I was truly ready to go public on this. I swallowed the lump in my throat, smiled gloriously, gushed my thanks, and had him adjust the clasp at my neck. I put on the earrings and as I turned around to model the combination, Theo was on the ground, kneeling with another identical box in his hand. I jolted in shock.

"Will you marry me Theresa Forrester? Tess. Come on. Let's do this. Be my bride?"

I burst into tears. Threw myself at him, hugging him, and we both ending up on the floor in his pub. "Yes. Most definitely!" I could hear the collective sigh of relief from everyone within a ten-mile radius, as he slid the ring on my finger. Phones were out clicking, text messages sent: "Yes! Finally." What did they mean "finally"? It had only been a few weeks. I guess that was my month. Theo opened a tab at the bar.

10.

Something changed almost immediately. Suddenly life went from being scrutinised, to being an out and out military invasion. Ahh. *This* is why I wanted some private space to savour the moment. Savouring was over. Everyone had an opinion on what a wedding should look like, or more specifically, what our wedding should look like. What my dress should look like; who the attendants should be; where the reception should be, and who should cater for it. And to be honest. I really didn't care. I had no illusions that I wanted a beautiful day, but I actually said yes to being with Theo, not just for a day but for my lifetime. That would go on even after all those things were done and dusted. The general opinion was that for a romance writer, I was not very romantic. I should have been way more excited.

I found all these well-meaning views quite oppressive. I wanted to scream and yell and tell everyone to go away and leave us alone. And then I realised, I had actually invited and strategized and insisted that these people interfere in my life. What was I thinking?

Joanie came over and sat down opposite me. It was Wednesday. I was hoping this was the last week of bathroom renovations so I could reinhabit my cabin during the week again. I had really wanted to spend this day writing. I was desperate to find out how Ben and Meg held together in that changing dynamic from workers to lovers. Was it going to be hard for them? I wanted to take courage from them as I worked out what this new season in our relationship was going to look like for me.

"So," said Joanie as she sat down and most seriously started to explain to me her social-media boards. "I have set up a board for reception décor, and another one for china settings, and bridesmaid dresses. Now we all know you look fabulous in deep colours and I look absolutely washed out pastels, so I think this is going to work out really fantastic."

I looked at her and couldn't think of anything to say, except something sarcastic about a swatch-match made in colour-heaven. I kept silent. Did she really think I would I go for my groom's ex-girlfriend in the bridal party? I pursed my lips and chose my usual tact: avoidance. "I haven't really decided on anything yet."

"Oh, of course. Absolutely necessary to look at all the ideas first. And I am a great researcher. My aunt wanted to buy a dog once. I shared so many photos and she picked out like the cutest puppy ever. She got this sweet little corgi. She loves her Lizzie-doggie so much."

The implication here was that Joanie was totally responsible for her aunt's canine bliss. Another assumption was that corgis were cute. I hadn't actually recognised this to be a reality outside Buckingham Palace. Dog's aside, the subtext also read that I should be bowing out, overwhelmed with awe by Joanie's incredible super-powers in web-browsing.

I shrugged. "I meant the bridal party... more than what they will wear."

"Oh."

"So, I'm not making any commitments with anyone just yet. I want to talk to each person first, before I let others know."

"Oh. Huh." She leant forward expectantly. "Well?"

I shrugged again. "Well what?"

"Well we can talk now. I have time."

Not likely Lady: you are not in my top ten. "I could. But like I said, I haven't decided yet." As I looked at her sitting there, she frowned and pouted, and then her narrow little face washed over with forbearance as if she suddenly realised, I was a third grader trying to learn to do cartwheels for the first time. I never actually thought it would be possible to feel condescension from Joanie. It seemed my incompetent tardiness was an affliction Joanie was destined to carry, and so she was waiting patiently for me to eventually catch up. She stared at me, tapping her long salon-painted nails, knowing that eventually I would acknowledge what the whole world already accepted as fact, and then finally, our wedding would be sorted to global satisfaction.

I was feeling very insecure about what scope I had to plan our wedding, as I wanted it. I was obviously deluded enough to think that the celebration of our marriage might vaguely, somewhat, in a remote sort of way, be about us.

11.

It is one of those things you have to do eventually: make contact with the priest to get the paperwork sorted. I drove past the few churches in town and chose the most appealing looking building. I made the appointment and rocked up with my pen ready. I was a bit surprised. He didn't look crinkled or deviant. He didn't wear a priest's dog-collar. Not even a tele-evangelists' three-piece suit and tie; or those strangulating black denims with a matching t-shirt and sports-jacket. That always looks a bit dodgy.

In fact, as he sat down in his normal inexpensive jeans and introduced himself as Sam, I was thinking that if I passed this guy in the street, I wouldn't look twice. I wondered if he would be the kind of priest who could marry us properly, and whether or not I should try a different church. Perhaps the way he spoke would shed light on his capability… or not.

"So," he said officially, "how can I help you?"

I explained our desire to get married locally and inquired whether he would be up for the job. He seemed to hesitate, and I seriously was having doubts, so I quickly asked, "You do have a license to marry?"

"Well, yes. Sure. I'm just wondering why you want to be married in a church."

"Oh. Well its simple really. I've always thought that a wedding in a little country church was a much more romantic notion than a registry office or a courthouse."

"Hmm. Well, we do have a local civil celebrant who uses some very tasteful venues, if you have no particular interest in God."

Oh. I had assumed a small community would not have a celebrant, and I wasn't keen on the expense of shipping one in. "God? What has this got to do with God?" As soon as I said it, I wanted to retract *that* question. Who in their right mind says that to a priest?

"Well for some people… nothing at all. For others… everything. I was just wondering where it was for you?"

"Oh." That was unexpected. I had no notion that I would be asked about God. I thought this was about myself and Theo. Didn't we figure anywhere in this equation?

"Well, we don't go to church. At least not your church. Actually, any church. But I'm not an atheist," I qualified quickly. "God is probably a very real idea for some people. I just have never considered it too much myself."

"Him." And he sort-of smiled.

"Sorry?" I missed what he said.

"Him. Well I do understand the pronoun doesn't have to be male, but it's the usual one. God is not an idea or an 'it'. 'He' is a way to help us appreciate that God is a real person: thoughts, feelings, personality, nature, conversation, life. So, I think you mean, 'you have not considered Him very much'."

"Really? Isn't it… he… like a Star Wars' life-force or something? How can you say that is a person?" Again, I groaned inside. Are you kidding me? I sounded like I had all the clarity of Joanie. That was an evil notion.

"Because you can't have a relationship with a force. Even a good force is still just impersonal energy. God's entire history

83

with people has been about relationship. Healthy relationship, broken relationship, having our relationship with God restored and learning to relate."

"So, you're saying unless I have a relationship with God, you won't marry us."

"Well, I could marry you. Like legally I can. I just don't see why you would want to. It would be like inviting a total stranger to be your best man. Doesn't sound very genuine. You strike me as genuine."

"You think so? Huh. I thought a priest would just want to make us attend church for a month, stop having sex and give a donation or something." I wanted him to be shocked and blush, because I said the word 'sex', and confessed to partaking. We were in a church after all.

"Yes, I guess that would be easier wouldn't it? Look. I'm very open to doing your wedding if that is want you want. But I want you to be sure. It sounds like you haven't really had much access to information about God, so why don't I give you some resources, and then you can come back and ask any sort of questions you want, before you invite God to your wedding?"

Sounded kind of strange, talking about God like that, but fair enough. "Sure." And I indulged myself with the idea of throwing some very clever, awkward, uncomfortable questions at the man so that he would just give in and marry us anyway. I really did like the look of his church. We could get some good photos there.

He handed me a book and a couple of pamphlets, and all the wedding handout information as well. We made another appointment time. Too easy. I would knock that all over pretty quickly. Then he said, "Can I pray with you before you go?" He shrugged. "I'm a pastor… it's kinda what I do."

"Oh well. Alright then." That was new. I'd never been prayed on before. "Do I have to kneel or something?"

He just smiled and said. "We are talking with God… just like we've been talking with each other. You've been very respectful sitting there talking with me, so I think that is fine."

"Oh. Okay." And suddenly I felt like a squirming two-year-old with a bladder problem.

He didn't seem to notice and hardly paused. "Gracious Heavenly Father, you have drawn this couple together… and they want to do life together. I ask that you continue to draw them to yourself, so that in finding each other they would also find you. Holy Spirit give them wisdom and insight as they explore this idea of a relationship with you and that you would bless them abundantly in every sphere of their lives. We ask this in the name of Jesus Christ our Lord, Amen."

I cleared my throat and said an emphatic "Amen." I felt very spiritual in that moment. I also wanted to get out of there quickly and write that prayer down. I could use that. It was really beautiful, and it touched something deep in my soul. Hard to explain how I felt just then.

He stood up and smiled as he shook my hand.

"What?" I asked. It seemed like he was sharing some sort of private joke… maybe with God… if they were relating as he suggested.

"Oh, it's just that you prayed a powerful prayer just now and I don't think you realised."

"Huh?"

"Amen. It means: 'So let it be. I agree. I want that.' You prayed that. I hope you do find what you are looking for." And I needed to get out of there.

Looking for? I didn't know anything was lost.

When I told Theo that I had met with the priest, he looked surprised. "You want to get married at the Catholic Church? Are you sure? Will they do that?"

"No... not the Catholic one... the one on North Street. I didn't know you were Catholic. I can get a quote from him as well I guess."

He looked at me and smiled a kind, indulgent smile. "I'm not Catholic. You haven't had too much to do with churches hey?"

"Nothing. Why?"

"Well most of them don't think of what they do as a commodity that they sell." He shrugged. "Perhaps some do... but most sort of go with the idea that religion is... I don't know... more about your soul."

"Yeah. That was the weirdest thing. This guy talked about a relationship with God. Look if you think this is not worth pursuing; he mentioned there is a local celebrant. I could check that out."

"No, I like the idea of getting married in a church. My mum would have liked that."

I had never heard him talk about his mother. And we snuggled a bit as he spoke about when he was growing up; how she was frustrated by his choices, and the things that happened

86

when he hit his teenage years... and then his marriage. Particularly the no kids... she had been looking forward to being a grandmother. "She said to me once. "I called you Theo, because it means 'God given'. You are a gift from God, Theo, and you will come back one day. I know that. I pray for that.""

"What did she mean by coming back? Back where?"

"Oh. She's talking about how I was as a kid. I grew up that's all. I've got some bookwork to do, so I'd better get cracking if I'm going to knock that over tonight." I checked a couple of other things I wanted to confirm with him, and then left him to it.

I drove back to the hut. That was the most unusual day I'd had in a long time. I felt so unsettled. Not rattled like Keith-rattled. This was a gentler sort of feeling... but it occurred to me that Sam might be right: something was missing. Not lost. I wouldn't go that far. Just missing.

12.

I sat down with Sam's material and a notepad, to record every question I had, so I could filter out the ones that had obvious answers. I felt totally uninformed about the whole thing. It was more than a bit embarrassing to realise my understanding of religious life was primarily an unfiltered view from sit-coms and cinema releases, very few of which were flattering. Maybe the Sound of Music was a little more respectful than most. Still, whatever my sources, I was religiously aware enough to know that Jesus was a bigot, and a brainwasher of weak-willed people who needed a prop. Just like Theo said: he out-grew it. Educated, well-adjusted people move on from that.

Except... Sam was a bit of an enigma. His whole presence was an interesting challenge to my Hollywood religion. He seemed open minded enough to continue the conversation. That, in itself, was curious. He didn't seem at all to have taken on the manner of the god he was supposed to be worshiping. He was kind and respectful. Uncanny.

I thought I would start with the questions I already had. I wrote down my ongoing social dilemmas about death, and pain, and child rape. But then there was also this idea of relationship. If God was a person I could relate to, then didn't that mean by definition he was human and not a god? Not much of a case for 'The God' no less. Why would people worship someone who was like them? Wasn't religion about a higher power, reaching for something bigger, outside yourself?

I opened the booklet and as I flicked through, it seemed to spend most of the time talking about Jesus. There was nothing about the Ten Commandments, which even I thought was a big omission. It occurred to me that Theo might be able to help since he grew up going to Sunday-school. When I asked him, he grinned and looked embarrassed, so I reassured him I was not converting. "Look I just want to get my head around it so that when I go back to this guy I don't seem like a complete idiot."

"I thought that was the point – to hit him up with questions."

"But I don't even know enough to ask good questions. Please just let me run a few things by you."

"Sure. Okay. Don't expect too much. That was a long time ago. You'll have to cross-check me."

"Okay. First question. In the Bible, who's Mark?"

"Don't actually know. Just some guy who wrote one of the gospels I think."

"Oh." That wasn't so helpful. "What's the gospel?"

"I remember that one. The word is supposed to mean "good news"… but it is actually the four books that were written about the life of Jesus. His biographies I suppose."

"So, Mark wrote a series of four of them?"

"No – just one. Matthew, Mark, Luke, and John. They are the four gospels. Each written by different people."

"So, which one is true?"

"Well they all are. Just a different take. More than one book has been written about Donald Bradman. Doesn't mean they aren't all valid from those perspectives."

"Huh. You remember a lot about this. Which one did you like the best?"

"Don't ever remember reading one beginning to end. Usually they'd just pick out verses and tell us what they meant."

"I've got the Gospel by Mark. It's only sixteen chapters; I'll be able to skim read that pretty quickly. You should too... so you know what I'm talking about when I ask you questions."

"Really?"

"Yes really. I am going to get this guy to marry us. So, read up and stop whinging. It will be good for us to talk about something intellectual for a bit."

Theo rolled his eyes. "You're excited because you've found a new author."

"No... I'm excited because I am going to get my way and be married in that church."

I sort of was shocked that I was reading part of a bible. It came straight to the point: "The beginning of the gospel about Jesus Christ", and I inserted Theo's meaning of "good news". Immediately I am introduced to a celebrity, someone who the people liked and wanted to be around. I didn't expect Jesus' willingness to be kind. One phrase sort of bugged me: Jesus presented "a new teaching... and with authority." I thought about that. Did it mean that Jesus was teaching something that they were not familiar with... and he did it without apology or hesitation? It seemed that if that was the case, he could back it up. Hmm. Where was the narrow-mindedness?

I asked Theo about the brainwashing bigot, he looked shocked. "Jesus is not like that. He never was. It's the church that is full of hypocrites." The way he said that, it sounded personal. It also struck me that the church was not the only institution that had a monopoly on not keeping their word, or being opinionated, or doing people over. I met customers, and professionals, and community figures like that every day.

So? This was confusing. I'm seeing a Jesus who was dynamic, considerate, able to hold his own with the contemporary political and religious experts of his era, supportive of the common people and their plights, willing to intervene and help... albeit with super-powers of healing and miracles. Perhaps it was too good to be true. Perhaps he was a historical figure that had been polished up to look better than he really was. Strange that I never doubted the ancient historical reality of Jesus. I was adept in cross-referencing data... and once I delved into the religious and historical reference points, there seemed a plethora of opinions covering both pros and cons. All were passionate: those against as well as the fors. It seemed impossible to stay neutral around Jesus. I found a statement I agreed with: *'when confronted with Jesus, he demands a response'*.

My neutrality about Christianity, up until now, seemed based on a gapping lack of information. I felt increasingly defensive as I read people badmouth Jesus, when it seemed pretty obvious, they had not actually read his story. I went online and downloaded the other gospels. This was an amazing story. He made so many claims and did so many genuinely good things and helped so many people. I realised with a genuine amount of grief, that I had also labelled him a religious and political extremist without even reading or knowing his story. Then I found an interesting letter from Martin Luther King Jr. written from prison. He said that Jesus was an extremist, but an extremist for love.

All through this exploration, Theo sort of went underground. He listened to my arguments, my questions, my bewilderment, as I discovered yet another point of view. Eventually he said two things. "You're getting yourself confused reading everyone one else's' opinion," and, "When are you going back to that minister guy. He'll be able to answer your questions better than me."

So, I made another appointment, and he asked that Theo come too. He was reluctant, but duly complied.

Sam sat on his lounge in a relaxed sort of slouch. "So how did you go with the information? Any questions?" It seemed like he genuinely didn't mind either way.

So, I asked how Jesus could get such bad reputation now-a-days, when it seemed like he did nothing to deserve the bad press. He shrugged and said, "It was no different when he was alive. Jesus actually asked those who accused him, which particular good thing they were condemning him for. Even at his trial they could not come up with anything that could stick. Except one thing... they said he claimed to be the Son of God. That meant he was claiming to be equal with God. That was blasphemy. They killed him for that one."

Huh. "So, if that is what Jesus is like, why are the people who follow him always plastered as hypocrites?"

Then he said, "It's a discerning distinction to make: separating the mistakes people make and the way Jesus is."

92

I smiled. "I'd like to take credit for that, but it was Theo who made me aware of it."

He turned to Theo who had gone a deep red. "Can we get on with the wedding info, because I have to get back to work," he said rather curtly.

Sam considered him briefly and said, "What did you want to know about the wedding?"

"Will you do it?"

"I will, if you want me to. Are you okay with inviting God to bless and challenge your marriage?"

"Challenge? I thought we would get a blessing... and the venue."

"I'm not licenced to sprinkle fairy-dust and wish happy thoughts. The Jesus you read about became involved in people's lives. He challenged their assumptions about the Kingdom of God. He is still alive today doing that same thing. That's what you are agreeing to. I'm not asking you to sign up to church membership. This is about you and Jesus. You are both on a journey to consider him... whether you call it that or not."

I sat there willing Theo not to get all high and mighty about this, and at least just say what the fellow was wanting.

He shrugged. "I used to think like that. When I was a kid. It's not that way for me anymore... I own a pub."

"Jesus had all sorts of people who did all sorts of jobs among his friends. Even publicans. I don't think it is about what you do... but about who you are."

"Damn."

"What?"

"Well... I've spent the last four years blaming my ex' for not thinking like that. That exact same thing."

"So, you wanted a Kingdom response from someone who didn't have Kingdom resources to deliver it? That's a big ask."

I felt like I was set in the middle of a gigantic maze and was supposed to find my way through it. "What do you mean by Kingdom? I have never heard people refer to religion like this."

"Jesus talked about the Kingdom of God. What that was like. How it works... what it means to be a follower of Jesus. He said the Kingdom of Heaven was like a loaf of bread, with yeast that rises slowly... changing... growing... transforming dough to bread we can cut sandwiches from. We can't expect kingdom bread from someone who is still flour. Not possible. And at the same time, often it is a slow process... hardly noticeable sometimes."

I felt myself drawn and repelled by the idea at the same time. Right then my concern was that I never wanted to wake up and discover I would abandon the man I love because of some frustrated ten-year plan. I needed to be Kingdom enough to stay. I had a compelling need to access those resources. "How do we get on this baking tray then?"

"You say yes. Tell Jesus you want to be in the Kingdom of God rather than out. Doing life with his resources: his way... with his strength... and his wisdom... and his courage... and his passion. The Holy Spirit will come, guide you, strengthen you... as you get to know Jesus more."

I looked at him and said emphatically, "Amen." That was a prayer I knew.

He tilted his head and smiled. "You want that?"

I nodded and avoided looking at Theo.

Sam smiled. "Well let's tell him then?" He waited for me to nod again, and then he quietly, gently spoke to Jesus about drawing me closer to the blue-print he had in mind when he created me. "Amen."

I didn't expect fireworks. I didn't expect anything actually... and I was surprised by unexplainable tears. Were they tears of relief, or embarrassment or joy, or regret? I couldn't explain it. And for someone who spent a lot of time at a computer keyboard articulating how people felt... this was a confusing place to be. A sacred moment: that's how Theo described our first Kiss. That was the closest thing I could think of. That described this for me. A sacred moment.

13.

Sam made another time to meet. He also said that there were lots of things to learn about doing life according to what Paul – whoever he was, called The Way. He said that church was a place to rub shoulders with others on this same road. "Some have good advice on what's ahead and can help us understand how to do this journey well. Some people are still just searching for answers, and some think they've solved every question ever asked and are not that helpful at all. Working out what works is part of the fun."

That made me smile. At least he wasn't telling me his church had perfected utopia. Just people learning, like me.

Relationship with God: I liked that thought. Not that long ago I was discovering what it was like to say I was somebody's girlfriend: in a relationship with Theo. Status – engaged. Now I could say the same about Jesus. It was something I also wanted to hold privately for a time. I didn't want to tarnish this with banter. In that Theo was absolutely right. It was sacred and I was sure someone would slam it or try and talk me out of it or tarnish it with argumentative opinions as if I was some on-line blog or chatroom. Maybe that was why I had wanted to keep our engagement private for a time. Certainly, bringing that out had been a painful process.

I realised that I had no trouble believing Sam's observation it was an illusion to 'expect Kingdom responses without Kingdom resources. It allowed the possibility that Jesus might not be too good to be true. If he was one who accessed Kingdom resources through his relationship with God consistently, perhaps it was possible he was as authentic and good and kind and wise as he was portrayed. It allowed that others who accessed those same spiritual resources might have the capacity to respond well in all sorts of situations also.

When I looked at my character of Ben through a fly-on-the-wall lens, it seemed every response since the duffing episode was how Jesus defined the values of the Kingdom of God. Blessed are the humble, the poor in spirit, the merciful, the peacemakers. Ben was appalled at Grossman's manipulation, and stoically refused to big-note himself. He patiently attended to Meg in her sickness; he didn't get mad at the trivial; or take his frustrations out on the cat; or be annoyed by the deficiencies in his simple world.

I thought of the characters I knew and loved in the books that I grew up with: the Annes, Janes, Lucys and the Elizabeths; the Darceys, Rochesters and the Paul-Emanuels. Their common ground of human weaknesses was a fair smattering of arrogance; their battle to overcome their flaws drove them to find peace with the people around them even through harsh experiences. Even Greek and Norse gods all had some Achilles heel. Why didn't Ben come out looking like that? Other characters I had worked with had significant imperfections, but not Ben. And yet he had no identifiable religious resources to help him be this person. Not that I knew of, anyway. It was the most unsatisfactory, incongruent aspect of my story, and my frustration was showing.

I noticed a shift in my own engagement with the ideas of God and Jesus... well – the persons of God and Jesus. So, if God is truly God, he was infinite; I could never box him in and I would never completely comprehend and know everything about who he is. How was it possible to 'out-grow' that? Rather it stirred in me a deep curiosity to see how much I could know: to see where the possibilities of this infinite love could take me. It was unexpected that I could not box God into a tidy little God-drawer and pull him out when it was useful. I must admit my relationship with God is the most inconvenient thing I have ever encountered. It pervades everything.

So now another question bugged me. What causes a follower of Jesus to end up some place else? If it's not about out-growing God, like some sort of toddler potty-training program, what happens? Is it boredom, or distraction, neglect, or hurt; or something else altogether? I wondered what happened to Theo. My sleuthing skills were on high alert, because whenever I broached the subject, the pile of invoices he needed to deal with, became urgent and all consuming.

On top of that, I had some well-meaning, off-beat women at church telling me that I should break my engagement with 'the publican', because well, I was above that now I went to church. Something about being unequally yoked. That was another discussion to have with Sam. Perhaps he wouldn't go ahead and marry us after all.

Thing is though, I was never marrying a publican, but Theo. And his choice of occupation did not define him. At least – that was what I wanted to believe. I wanted to be above his ex' who abandoned the occupation and the lifestyle, with little consideration of the person. That was my initial motivation for starting this thing with God in the first place. I wanted to believe that, like Jesus, I could love people who were the tax-collectors and prostitutes, rather than write them off because of their jobs. Although to be honest, if I was going to marry someone, I would have an issue with that oldest profession. Couldn't get past that one. Made a publican seem very respectable.

Would God lure me into starting a relationship with him by wanting to have the capacity to love stronger, and then, would he demand I pull the pin on Theo because he didn't change, and I had? That didn't make sense to me. Did I want Theo to be on the same page when it came to my relationship with God? Of course. I prayed for that. Still he flatly would not talk about it or give any indication of an allegiance to Jesus, outside the respect that he had for his mother who believed "that stuff". And yet he honoured my choice, even if he didn't share that part of me. Would it be okay if he never did? Wow. I was so confused.

Was I perpetuating this deception by telling Ben's story? It seemed I was completely expecting Kingdom responses from a man who refused to acknowledge Jesus – the sovereign of that Kingdom. How could he go from felon to faithful just like that? Was I suggesting it was possible to be like Ben, solid enough, just by being the right sort of person, to respond consistently, unrealistically, without any outside resources to do this as a normal, fallible person? And then, if you're not the right sort of person, how could you ever be held accountable for behaviour that hurts? Surely you would be exempt from those consequences if you were just a victim of unfortunate genetics or social fall-out.

As I thought about Ben – I started to hate him. He was a phoney, an illusion, a fake, a paper-cut-out character. And I despised Meg for not seeing through him. But I honestly had to admit this was how the story was unfolding. I saw him no other way. Was I judging Ben without knowing his back-story? I was experiencing the fear I sensed in Meg when she realised she had no idea who he was… and their relationship could seriously ricochet off in any direction. And that fear echoed in my love for Theo.

In the past, I had no trouble trusting the knots in a story would unravel in the end. But I worried that this time it would not come together. It was a fundamental issue that if it were never resolved, it would make this whole exercise in storytelling impossible to see the light of day. How pointless! It felt a whole lot like Meg carrying her pregnancy that would never be viable. How dare Ben jeopardise my sabbatical writing retreat, through his unlikely excellence! That was not fair. Totally not fair.

It seemed then my story evaporated. I sat with Ben and Liam working on the farm in freeze frame for over a month. Where I could once pick up the thread of their story in a moment, I now looked at them building their shed, watched by Meg knitting baby clothes on the verandah and I seriously had no idea when that next conversation would occur. I couldn't hear what they were saying. I couldn't see what they were seeing. I tried to pan out in my mind and get the larger view, but there was nothing except them walking along the track with a barrow full of stone, and then they seemed to disappear through some science-fiction star-gate and vaporise.

I would doze off and jolt awake and put myself to bed, to try and meet up again on the morrow. But the next day was the same… and the next. I didn't feel motivated to force it, and when I did try to push through, I sat there staring at my computer, and eventually found myself distractedly flicking through social media posts.

I've had my fair-share of blocked moments, but this seemed more severe and more terminal than anything I had encountered before. It made the Keith episode seem like merely stalling at traffic lights. Now I was facing a blown gasket or cracked engine-block. I can change a tyre, but perhaps this was a serious breakdown. A crash. A write-off. Irretrievable. I had no idea what to do.

I set aside my computer and went to work on wedding preparations. Joanie was relieved that I had finally got serious about planning arrangements. She 'ooh-ed' and 'ahh-ed' over flowers and beads and tulle and ribbon. She brought out a selection of samples of stationery card and paper and gold pens and glitter and bell-shaped split-pins with other craft essentials. I couldn't have hired a more enthusiastic assistant if I had thousands of dollars to buy the employed devotion of a wedding planner. So, I rolled with her ditsy giggles, and her annoying expert airs, and felt so sad that my characters had gone AWOL.

Theo sat down one afternoon and smiled indulgently at Joanie's collection of colour swatches that sat neglected on the table, pushed aside as I ate.

"Having fun?" he said, pointing to the pile of fabric samples.

"Sure. I'm thinking claret. Very 'pub'."

He grinned. "You do know you don't have to go with Joanie's authoritative opinion on everything."

"This one is mine. I'm happy with it."

"Cool. Just as long as it's your choice. She can be pushy."

"Joanie? Pushy? Are we talking about the same person?"

"You okay? You seem pensive. Is this getting to you?"

"The wedding prep? Na. I'm okay." And I picked up my coffee mug just a little   quickly. "You and Joanie. She said you had a "thing" going once. Was that a long time ago?"

Theo considered me for a moment and sighed. "It lasted long enough for me to privately refer to it as a Category 4 cyclone during my summer-from-hell. My head wasn't in the right place, and my heart wasn't even in play."

"She talks about it like you and her have this long-term connection." Of course, Joanie would advertise that as credibility to be involved in the wedding.

"She thought I was her prince in shining armour, and all she got was a broken-down foot solider. And since Joanie doesn't have the Nightingale qualities needed to walk the rounds of a Crimean War hospital, I had to find another way to heal. Just then I was a mess. It was never going to last."

"Touching analogy. I still think she wants this to be her wedding. She's possibly still in love with you."

"She loves being in the lime-light, that is all." I thought he was going to say something else. But he closed his mouth and kissed my cheek as he went back to his office. I wished he had said something more, well… anything.

It was about then that I had another thought… a thought that seemed quite random, but it really started freaking me out. What if God didn't like me writing? What if this writer's-block was God's way of telling me I shouldn't write because my stories were too carnal or unspiritual or something bad like that? If I was a Christian, my writing should probably now be filled with repentant prayers and pithy sermons and bible verses imbedded in every page. This was not how the story was unfolding, but did that mean I should go back and edit in an appropriate amount of religious content, just to make it properly Christian? I hadn't been doing this long, but I assumed that this was what it meant to be a Christian writer.

I sat with Sam, and looked across the coffee table at him. "I have a question for you."

He grinned. "I don't ever remember anyone taking me up on the "ask me any question" challenge quite as enthusiastically as you have."

"So, you regret that open door policy now? Do you want to rewrite the contract?"

He grinned. "I love sitting with the questions. I like the idea that God said, *'Come on, sit down and let's reason this out together.'* I try to remember good questions never intimidate God. He designed us to think intelligently about life."

I took a breath. "You were saying about this idea of God fundamentally changes the way we look at our world… changes our DNA… how it impacts our worldview. Yes? And that God is not compartmentalised into only certain parts of our life; he is not limited to just particular relationships or reserved for designated conversations. God is everywhere. This is who we are… so everything we do becomes a 'Christ expression' of our life. All of my life becomes Christian, not just me on Sunday doing certain religious things." Sam looked sort of amused or relieved, that I had remembered what he had said. So, I continued. "That means we are now having a Christian wedding... and we have a Christian pub so to speak ... and we are a Christian couple."

"Is Theo on board with this? Has he made a decision?"

"No. Not yet. I'm not speaking for him... just my part in this. Besides, I was reading the story in the Bible of that kid who ran away from home to party and ended up a pig-farmer. Theo told me his mother prayed before she died and told him he would come back home. I didn't know what she meant when he told me that, but I get it now. I have no reason to doubt it. His mother didn't."

Sam shook his head, kind of amazed.

"What?"

"I've realised part of me wants to instil a level of faithless realism into your brand-new perception of life. But something is holding me in check. Certainly, we can't allow our Christianity to rubber-stamp any behaviour if it is not congruent with what Jesus demonstrated as Kingdom living. But I don't think you are saying that. What I hear you saying is that you will do your bit and God will do his. This is the child-like faith I insist on every Sunday. I preach for it; I argue for it; I pray for it.... And yet when I see it, it seems my reaction is to shut it down. You have shown me something in my own life. I've forgotten how to step out of the boat."

"Sorry?"

"It's from the story where Peter got out of a fishing boat in the middle of a storm and walked over the water to Jesus. Here; read it for yourself... that event is metaphorical of our faith journey on so many levels," and he scribbled the reference on a piece of paper and handed it to me.

I took it and stuffed it in my pocket anxious to ask away before I lost my nerve. "Anyway. My problem is this: the DNA thing means I am also a Christian writer. But nothing has changed in the way I write. I don't write religiously, I just write. Does that mean I can't do it anymore? I don't know how to do it any other way..." I took a deep breath and frowned. "Oh."

"Oh? What 'Oh'?" Sam was concentrating, following my musings.

"I have had the biggest case of writer's block ever. I was thinking it might mean that God does not want me to write any more. But now I think I just need to find a way of doing it 'Christianly'... the process. I thought I had to put sermons in it, or prayers... which I have done by the way – plagiarised a lot of what you have said, if I am honest. But it is more than that. The *way* I write needs to reflect my new DNA... then the story will contain that same DNA – it will automatically have the mark of the Kingdom because it is birthed from my DNA, which I get from my Father. That is a very reassuring idea." Sam looked across at me sort of shaking his head, but not in a negative way. I smiled at him and stood to my feet. "Thanks Sam. I think that answers my question."

He grinned. "Any time. Happy to explore Kingdom with you. It is a great place to live."

14.

Write Christianly? I didn't actually know if that was a thing, but Sam was not terribly shocked by my conclusions, so I took courage from that. What would that look like? Could it apply to fiction... or only spiritual self-help manuals and bible-study dissertations? There was this niggling sort of idea that came from a conversation I had after church one Sunday with a man who had no clue what I did. After some polite small-talk, I alluded to the fact I had moved here to take some time-out to write. He frowned and asked the usual questions: was I published; what titles had I written, and then, instead of taking the line of conversation by asking about my style or genre, he demanded to know the subject of my speciality.

"What speciality subject?"

"You know... subject. What part of the Bible do you focus on? Everyone has a pet subject."

"Oh." I raised my eyebrows. Everyone? I didn't know that. And of course, I noted that only Bible subjects counted. "I actually write fiction."

"Really? Not biographies? Not theological subjects?"

"Nope. Just pretend stuff; made up mostly, often loosely based around some historical event or setting usually. People's lives... relationships under pressure... how they get through."

Where most people at this point in a conversation, will tend to smile wide-eyed and congratulate me on my creative ambitions, he looked at me as if I was some sort of social-retard, who needed to grow up, take out my pigtails and wear my hair up in a sensible bun. "Huh. What a waste of time," he muttered as he walked away. I watched him zero in on some other person who potentially was deeper and more sincere; and who apparently wasn't a waste of his time.

As I walked back to the pub, I was smarting under his judgment and I found myself producing a kind of literary caricature in revenge:

> *"The little man bent over his mug; his hooked nose protruding, carefully sniffing out something, anything, worthy of his condescension. His dark brow gathered in a frown as he gagged on his milky tea. Offended, his nose wriggled uncomfortably. Something had the distinct odour that was suspiciously beneath him. Frivolous! Puerile! He abruptly left to find a more worthy recipient of his presence. A Regent, resplendent in regalia uniform, could not have been more pompous in a parade among street urchins."*

I smiled at my little foray into spite. I did feel a little better, even if it did mean identifying with street urchins. Actually, I was not too uncomfortable with the thought of associating with the disenfranchised. What I really wanted to know was not whether my preference for fiction was wasting his time, but God's time. The lack of free-form creativity that academic essays demanded drained me. Of course, I could write formally, I'd done my degree in Tourism, but I actually enjoyed doing this. Who was he to slight the value of what I loved, even if it wasn't his thing? I wasn't asking him to read anything I produced. So why was I so upset by the opinion of someone I didn't know, who would never read what I wrote, even briefly enough to form a considered opinion? I couldn't answer that, and it didn't stop me being very disturbed by his condemning verdict of frivolousness.

I sat at the counter with a coffee and told Theo about his callously aired opinion.

"You're not really surprised, are you? It had to come. You are marrying a Publican. You are never going to fit in."

"First. I'm marrying you and not your pub... even if it has your name on the door."

"Yeah. But I come with the job. It's not to everyone's taste. Don't I know it."

"But this wasn't even a conversation about who I am engaged to or what he did for a living. We were just talking about writing. And then he got all high and mighty about subject matter. Why would writing about people and how they do life... how they struggle, and find meaning, and search for acceptance... how can that be a bad thing? It explores these common human experiences. I think I want to instil hope that 'purposeful' has many different faces, and the search for those essential core desires crosses time. Someone may identify with my character's struggle and be encouraged to keep going in their own search."

Theo looked at me then. "Are you disappointed that I have never read anything you've written?"

"I might be... a little... that you have never asked me about it much. Guess I assumed it was not your thing. At the same time... I kind of took it for granted that you thought I write well enough for my readership and that was sufficient. That was a sort of comfortable idea."

"Does it matter whether your good at it or not? You're doing what you love."

"Well it does really. I want to believe I'm doing something well enough that it entertains and encourages and inspires."

"You know, I think I would like to read about these people who have consumed so much of my fiancé's time."

"Yeah but... the stories are girly. No gun fights, explosions, car-chases. I don't do any of those. Different pace. You are really not going to like it. Besides, I'm not done, and I don't show until I'm finished."

"So, you've already judged whether I'm a suitable reader, and you're not going to let me see it?"

"Perhaps I don't want you to tell me it's a waste of time too."

He grinned at me. "You are scared."

"Might be. And even if I am, I don't see how that is funny."

"I don't think you get it. You could write crap... and it wouldn't matter an iota to me. You like doing it. Someone will read it... but even if they don't, it's the person who you are while you are writing that I love. I have watched you get edgy, pace, smile and cry. Whoever these people are that you write about, you love them. They make you care."

"I kind of feel that I should be caring for real people."

"You do. I'm real – you care for me."

"So, you don't think it is a waste of time."

"What if others can connect to them like you do? Perhaps that builds empathy and understanding. That can't be a bad thing. The world can always do with more empathy."

"You present a rather heart-warming case. I could marry you."

"I really want to Tess," said Theo rather self-consciously, "...even though they might throw you out because of your disgraceful publican."

"Throw me out? Out of the church? You forget I feel comfortable there." He never came with me to check it out. Was he judging the church-story without reading it as well?

"Yeah, but it won't last."

"Why not?" I was a little defensive.

"Because eventually they will give you the flick. Basically, you and me, we are not good enough." Ahh. There it was again. The street urchin... and the high and mighty Regent.

"Well, I've already been told I should break my engagement. And I haven't taken on that advice."

"See. I told you. Did Sam tell you to shut me down?"

"No of course not. He's doing the ceremony. Don't think he'd spring that on us as I'm walking down the aisle."

"Who then?"

"Oh, a couple of people. Well, one lady in particular. I don't know her... and she doesn't know me... so be reassured, I'm not going to take any advice from her." Funny how I could filter out those comments about us, but this little judgment on my writing... that was really bugging me.

15.

I sat at my table and stared at the stone wall that was my living room and the rough timber windowsill, worn and aged, that looked out over the paddocks. Stone upon stone. I imagined Ben laying the mortar. Positioning the rocks. Checking the string line. I imagined Meg sitting in the shade of the forming wall, fanning her face, holding her growing body, swelling from pregnancy. Shifting her weight, she held her abdomen in an embrace, almost too scared to believe… hoping beyond hope that this time it would be okay. Would it be possible that this time she could be a family?

I sat with that fear for a long while. I felt it. My stomach churned. I knew this fear… because it was my fear. Not of a pending delivery of course, but of marriage. Would it be okay this time? Would it come through… or would it be cut short… again?

Damn.

I have not been honest.

I had not told Theo about this.

I had not wanted to speak about it in case by doing so, I would unleash a whole lot of demons who would work to destroy something beautiful.

I picked up my phone and sent a message. *We need to talk. Now.*

I knew he would come. Of course, he would. And he did. It took him a couple of hours, but such is the life of a business owner. I was glad of the delay. I paced, and prayed I'd be strong enough to follow through. After all, I had made some very confident declarations about being a person with follow through. I almost expected that this aspect of my character would be challenged. It seemed to happen that way.

He drove up and the dust settled. I heard his tread, and I felt fear rise up to choke me. Would it happen again? How could I be sure that this time it would be different?

He came in and looked at my face. He swore and flicked on the jug. This was a cup of coffee sort of conversation. He said nothing… but I read fear in his eyes as well. My fear was becoming his fear.

He sat down and handed me my mug. He stared at my eyes trying hard to push down the panic that I saw hovering there. I said nothing to reassure him, because what I had to say could well be a deal-breaker. But I could no longer just pretend it wasn't part of my story.

I swallowed.

"Theo, I need to apologise. I haven't been completely honest. But I want to tell you something, and I need you to listen and not interrupt. Please. This is not easy for me."

I *felt* him swear. He didn't say anything out loud, but I felt his dread. In a strange way his fear felt like having a comrade at arms… someone who understood my terror because he was sensing it too.

Stone upon stone. Start at the beginning.

"I told you I moved here to write. Which of course is true. But in a sense that was only part of it. I also came here to get away; to focus on doing something different. And I don't think it is fair to expect someone share their life with me when they don't know this part of my story. I want you to know this… well, this 'ugly' part of me. I have been pretending it was another person, another life… that the fairy-tale will play out, but perhaps it won't. And I feel I need to allow you to make that choice… and not me do it for you. I need you to know this side of what you are getting if you marry me."

Theo's eyes locked into mine.

"I was in a relationship before I came here. We had been going well. We were getting married. I was engaged… informally. Committed without a ring or without ever setting a date… always believing that it would happen any day. And then I got pregnant. The day I found out was the worst day of my life. Phil panicked. I couldn't make a decision. I was counselled to…" I closed my eyes and my words rasped in my dry mouth. "I was counselled to… like it was taking a tablet for an inconvenient headache. I didn't know what to do. Phil suddenly became really distant. He suddenly became indispensable at work. He suddenly was imposed upon for a lot of work trips away. He suddenly decided to have an affair. My life was falling apart, and I couldn't comprehend how I could possibly be a mother. I could not see how I could do that.

I listened to the experts and not to my heart. So, I did it.

And I hate myself for doing it.

I hate that I didn't have the courage to at least see the pregnancy through and let someone else be her mother.

I hate that I need to tell you, and now you know this about me.

I hate that I wasn't honest with you.

But you made me forget. You were like anaesthesia for me. You told me I was content. And I was. I had convinced myself that my heart was untouchable. That I could live vicariously through my stories, that real relationships were not needed because they were too risky; that real family was not safe enough. But then you made me feel safe, and when you are around, I feel beautiful... and loveable... and it feels like that other stuff has never happened, and that it was inevitable we'd be together... like destiny. I hadn't realised how discarded I felt by Phil leaving like that. You changed all that. I finally had my own story that was lovely and untainted. Suddenly I was desirable, and I belonged.

But it freaked me out... and it seemed like if I made a big deal about your flaws, then the attention would be off mine, and this part of me would never be discovered... and no one need know. I convinced myself that you particularly didn't need to know. I had got rid of the pregnancy, and I buried the truth. But as the wedding gets closer and closer, this refuses to stay covered: it's been shuffling closer and closer and closer to the surface... and I can't keep it hidden anymore.

My characters are conflicted about being honest with their partners and showing both their good side and their ugly bits, but I haven't had the integrity to do the same. I'm really sorry Theo, and I totally get if you want to finish this now."

He sat back against the lounge. He stared at me while the tears fell from my eyes. I guess I knew then it would end here. My heart was breaking again. Could mistakes ever be out lived? In my heart I screamed at God to help me not to go under again.

"That's it?" he said eventually.

"What do you mean?"

"Anything else?"

114

"Kind of think this is enough. I have blood on my hands. I feel like Lady Macbeth, that the spots cannot be washed away."

"Well, I want to believe this wouldn't be an option when I'm in your life. But even if it was… at least I would like to think you wouldn't be alone in having to sort through such a decision. And… I thought the whole point about forgiveness is that it is forgiven. At least that's what my Mum used to say."

I shook my head. I felt afraid. I obviously had not heard right. "I don't understand…"

"Think you do."

"But I thought you would hate this about me."

"Why? I love you."

"Theo… how can you say that? I fully expected you to throw the book at me. How can you forgive something so monumental? Don't you think it is important? What I did is *not* okay! I didn't expect this."

"It is what it is… but I don't think it is the unforgiveable sin," he said soberly.

I searched his face, looking for a hint of retribution, or disgust, or judgment… and what I saw were echoes of deep sadness. But even in the failure there was a profound sense of hope. Perhaps…

"What you said about forgiveness, I would expect Jesus to say something like that. Sam said kingdom responses without kingdom resources is not possible."

"He said it was a big ask."

"That is true. He did say that." And my heart sunk. Theo had evidently made a kind of bravado resolution to do better, try harder… but alone, without God. I was struggling to find my own place with God as I acknowledged this part of my life. And in the process, I had just driven a wedge deeper between him and God. More failure. More church people letting him down. It was moving him further away from God… not closer. I never meant to be part of that.

"Tess, I don't know what to say. It is not fair you had to make that decision. This is as much on your ex, as on you. Am I shocked? Sure. I didn't know about this… or your ex. But in a way – I'm relieved that you recognise it was awful. It would be worse if you just thought it was a routine thing that didn't mean anything."

"Damn it, Theo! You are seriously messing with my head. Why don't you need God?"

"Who says I don't?"

"Well you did…"

"I did?"

"I think so. Don't you?"

"Pretty sure I do."

"You do? You do what?"

"Need God. Yeah I need him."

"You do? Are you sure?"

"Yeah. Pretty sure."

"I'm sorry. I'm confused. You do or you don't?"

"I do."

"You do? And when were you going to tell me this?"

"I don't know. It's kinda personal… but it was getting to the point where I couldn't 'not tell' anymore. Like this. It was coming to the surface I guess."

"But my thing is shameful. God is supposed to be a good thing. Why wouldn't you tell me?"

116

"Scared maybe. Was reading about that guy Nicodemus who met Jesus: at night; when no one was around; so no one would know. He was an undercover believer. So, my fear is not new. Nor is my way of handling it."

I sat there stunned. The thing I had been hoping for and praying for was just there. No fanfare. No weepy scenes of repentance; no lightning bolts of revelation. I wondered if I felt ripped off because it wasn't dramatic. "What happened? How did you know?"

"It's been creeping up on me. I think when you said you had decided not to leave, even though they were telling you that you should... that gave me hope it is possible to think independently – and not be micromanaged by 'the church'. That's what I hated – the whole intellectual suicide part of it... being told how to think, what to do, how to do it. I bucked against that. Never thought that was right. I always thought God should add to our capacity to think things through, not take it away. That was my biggest reason for giving up on it. The sheep thing. More like lemmings."

"Oh."

"That... and they were pretty nasty about it. Whenever I didn't conform or if I dared to question anything... it got nasty. That didn't sound like the Jesus I knew. He had some pretty robust conversations. So, I figured I got him wrong. When you said that about Jesus being a bigot, I was surprised by my response. I didn't even think about it, it was just there... like it was my default setting. It made me think I wasn't wrong about Jesus, but the way they handled my questions was. That isn't Jesus being offensive. Can't blame him for their bad behaviour. They have their own choices to make on how they follow him."

117

"We never spoke about that day in Sam's office. I was afraid you might not approve."

"The first thing I thought was Mum would be sitting up in Heaven having a cup of tea, having the biggest joke about it. Then I thought maybe it was a phase; but after a while I got that it wasn't. It's changed the way you see things. You were asking questions, and that didn't freak Sam out. He was encouraging you to ask and explore the answers. I liked what I saw there. It added to the process… didn't shut it down or subtract from it. More of the same idea."

"Huh. You know some people have been telling me to break up because we were "unequally yoked", but you could have as easily dumped me because we were thinking differently as well. Yet you didn't."

"When you sent me that message this afternoon, I really thought this conversation was going to be that. I was so sure it was inevitable… that you were going to tell me we were done. Having an abortion is a sad thing… but I think I would have found the other harder."

"Thank you for hearing me out." I sat for a while and just looked at him. "If you were so scared, I'd leave… why didn't you just tell me you believed?"

"What? You wanted me to lie about it?"

"Well no… but you could've eased my mind some, when you started to."

"Well, by then it seemed irrelevant. You said you would stay. Rather than trying to force my hand or give me an ultimatum… you were just waiting. It felt like you knew God would get through to me."

"I wasn't just 'waiting'… I was praying too. What your Mum said made the difference for me. She believed it, even though she never saw it. That's incredibly powerful stuff." I leant over and kissed him. I ran my hand over his back and up under his shirt. He firmly placed his hand on mine, arresting my caress.

"You know this is not right, hey?"

"You never objected before."

"Never spoke up about following Jesus before either. We're not married yet, so I'm going to sound quite insane and say we're going to wait. Which means I'd better go, because if you keep looking at me like that, I'm not going to hold out. I want to do this his way now."

"Seriously?"

"Yep. Serious." He stood up and picked up his keys. "Thanks for being honest with me Tess. Not long now; and I will be your husband." And he kissed my forehead and walked out. It was the hottest thing… seeing a man choose the harder thing, just because he believed it was right.

I sat with a pile of cards and put down the gold-tip pen. I went into Theo's office. "So, who do I put down as Joanie's Plus-One? Mick or Ted?"

"Why would you put down Mick or Ted?" he asked.

"That's why I'm asking. I don't want to put the wrong name on the invite."

"Oh…"

"Oh? What do you mean 'Oh'?"

"Well… I thought you knew that Mick was…well… like a client. A regular. Ted is too."

"Clients?" A vague sort of unease started to spread across my chest.

"Yes. Joanie is… well, you know… a worker."

"A worker. Like a *worker*?"

He nodded.

"Why didn't you tell me she was a hooker?" I whispered viciously.

"Well because I thought you knew… and I didn't think it mattered if you didn't."

"You don't think that matters? I was considering having her in the bridal party!"

"If you want to, you still can. Shouldn't make any difference."

"It makes a difference to me." I felt like I wanted to fumigate my colour swatches for gonorrhoea. I gasped as another thought hit the radar screen of my mind. "You! Were you a client?"

"You mean did I pay? No. But like I said the other day… she expected me to be her Richard Gere. I wasn't that person, so it ended."

"You went out with a hooker!"

"We stayed in mostly."

"Oh, my goodness I really have to think about this. I don't know where to go with this. Not at all." I rubbed my hand over my forehead. Not real. Not real. Country towns don't have workers. They are in big cities, and continental down-town districts. I looked over at Theo who was sitting there in an uncomfortable sort of way, his hand on his chin. "What?"

"You're freaked out by that. You didn't know the first thing about a church before you came here. And yet now you're spinning out because a sex worker seems like a normal person."

"This is not about church. I would have had the same issue before. I just don't agree with this... career choice. Come on Theo. You can't think this is just like working at the grocery store!"

"Obviously not. It put a pretty firm end to our relationship. But I'm not going to pretend that I've got any right to be the moral police here just because the girl chooses that."

"Why not? It's not right."

"Well to start with, the girl is not Kingdom. She doesn't have either Kingdom standards, resources, or motivation to do anything about it. As far as she's concerned, she's got a well-paying gig, with good hours. She controls her own bookings and isn't pressured into taking clients she doesn't want. It's not like she's a sex-slave."

"Still doesn't make it right. She doesn't have to."

"Different issue, I think. Don't think for a moment I'm okay with it, because if you are thinking of a career change, we are done. But everything you've been saying about Kingdom, here is a real live example of how we do that."

"Well it seems like you're very okay with it. She's your friend."

"I am okay with her... as a friend."

"Where's the line?"

"Yeah… where is it? Not okay with her job; not something I'd want my sister or my daughter doing, and not someone I want to marry. What do you want me to do? Tell her she can't come into the pub anymore?"

"Well maybe not be so chummy…"

"Chummy? What does that even mean? Which lifestyle choice do I remove myself from?"

"I just never expected to have to deal with this. Is this what owning a pub is like? Having to turn a blind eye to people's destruction?"

"I think this is what being human is like. Wherever we go people are in a fluctuating state between healthy and destructive. Four years ago, I was a bomb on a short fuse and how I didn't detonate I'm not really sure. But I do know it wasn't people turning a blind eye and leaving me to it that helped me get through. It was Ramon coming in and doing more than his fair share. It was Joanie taking a shift when the casuals couldn't come in. It was each patron still giving me business and telling me they appreciated that I stayed."

"They said that?"

"Well… mostly they'd just abuse my ex and order another drink. You get to know what people mean."

"Doesn't answer the question."

"I'm just saying that when I was in a state of destruction, it was people being around that helped, not them putting me in quarantine or going on about how I needed to pull my life together. Just then, I didn't care whether I blew up or not."

"Well it is sort of different. You were the victim then."

"Really? Depends on who you ask. According to my ex' she was the victimised one." He shrugged. "She might be right."

"So, you think I should ask Joanie to be in the bridal party?"

"No. Why? She doesn't get concessions for poor lifestyle choices."

"God I'm confused."

"Tess… just be yourself. That's all you have to do. Stick to how you want to do it. If you want her in, include her. If you don't, don't. When someone wants to talk about why you make the choices you do… tell them then. But their choices are not contagious. You didn't turn gay, just because you ate Ramon's food. You haven't become a hooker because Joanie gave you her opinion on stationery options."

"Not the same as an STI."

"Gossips, gluttons, addicts, adulterers, gay, straight, sex workers, shop lifters, grand larceny, tax avoiders, or just being nasty when someone disagrees. None of us gets to throw the first stone. That's what Jesus said. He hung around with hookers too. He even included me… a publican. And none of us ever compromises who he is."

16.

I realised that I didn't want Ben and Meg's story to have a happy-ever-after when such a reality was so elusive in real life. In this story I was okay with the tragedy of cancer in the prime of life, widowhood, the loss of a premature, deformed baby with spina-bifida and multiple life-threatening problems. There was a string of tragic tales resting in the Petrea Downs graveyard: some named, some unmarked, nameless and unacknowledged. Each seemed a reasonably appalling tragedy. But why should Meg and Ben hold a happy ending? Why should they have something normal? Why should their family be blessed? That was not fair. Life was not fair.

It was true: I resented my own version of heartbreak. Even with Theo in my life, I had no confidence that it was possible for life to be reclaimed after mistakes. My mistake. What was forgiveness anyway? Even when Theo could so confidently assert pardon was available, I had to acknowledge the fact that these consequences could not be wiped. Not for the... foetus. That is what they called it. Just a pregnancy. No acknowledgement. It stayed de-identified. But I was not fooled. It bore the brunt of my decision.

Oh.

Baby.

I never named my baby. It had been too early to tell of course whether it was a girl or boy... but it sat like a nameless vacant space in my life. My baby. I was told it was a procedure. I was told it had risks. But I was never told of grieving protocols for abortions. Even as I write that, it sounds hard, cold, clinical, hateful, impersonal, cruel.

I threw down the pen that I had been using to doodle on a pad and walked outside. I stood on the cobblestone pavers that made the path to my door and looked out over the paddocks. Nothing seemed different from yesterday, but as I stood there, I had awareness that today was different from yesterday, and that tomorrow would be different again from today. Nothing stayed the same. Ever. Lives are born. Lives are taken away.

What was different about today? Today I name my baby. Naming is a process I'm familiar with. I spend a lot of time choosing names. I name characters; creations made to fill a void in a story. Although, I admit I didn't really choose Meg's name. As soon as I had seen the formal inscription 'Magdalena' on that gravestone, she was always Meg. Her name fitted so well the moment she stormed through the doorway that first day I sat down and started to write. Likewise, Ben had always been Ben. Alistair's name went through a number of versions because what I chose never seemed strong enough for what he endured. I would search for a name on the web, just to see what would come up. Grossman also went through a number of edits. I needed a name that I felt no connection to. And whenever I remembered someone I admired or liked with the latest version of his name; I would change it... again. It was like changing socks.

So, what about this? What name would connect with all that was as special as a baby? A baby. My baby. Not a character in a plot. Not a script. Not an imaginative friend or foe; not a foetus; not a bunch of cells... but life. Real life. Human life.

Life I created. Life I was intended and mandated to protect. I stood there and tears welled. What did I hope for her, now that I recognised her part in my life... her own life? Or his?

What I wanted... what I really wanted was life to come out of the ashes... like the legend of the phoenix: life and strength and beauty rising out of something that consumed and destroyed. Ash. So... Ashley. Boy or Girl. Whether or not the web-sites agree with the meaning of the name or not... it was what I believed for her... him... that there will be a beautiful exchange... beauty for ashes; the strength of a tall Ash tree, where there had only been weeds and bent, broken reeds. If my surname, Forrester, was named for a worker of the forest... what sort of forest did I want my family to be known for? What part of the King's forest would we tend? I sat outside and looked out over the paddocks and wrote Ashley a letter: a letter of sorrow, a letter of apology, a letter of hope. And in writing I felt that perhaps I would get to believe those things for myself as well.

I watched Theo pour a glass of wine as I put down our meals. He smiled as we sat and said Grace. It was a way of welcoming Jesus to our meal; the third unseen guest at our table. I read that somewhere. Initially I thought it was a bit creepy, like the surveillance of a spiritual stalker on a stakeout to catch us out. But now I thought of it more like including our friend, a valued member of our family, a brother, a wise family uncle. Of course, he would be welcome.

We had this ritual of recapping our day. Positive conversations. Confrontation and difficult subjects were not allowed at the meal table; they were to be discussed at other times. I broke the rule. "Theo," I said quietly as I swirled my wine, looking at the ripples of red. "What do you think about kids?"

"Kids? Whose kids?"

"Ours."

He went really quiet. He put down his glass, and stared at mine, as I took a sip. Eventually he asked very quietly, "Are you pregnant? I know we haven't for a bit... but..."

Oh. That was kind of awkward. I laughed nervously. So, he didn't want this. The lack of kids from his marriage was evidently an ongoing choice. His mother, if she were alive, would still be disappointed. "Well no. Not that I know of. Wouldn't be drinking this if I was."

"Huh." He picked up his knife and fork, and focused very hard on his steak, cutting it very slowly.

My appetite left. I used my fork to play with the peas, rolling them around my plate like I was sorting tiles for a mosaic of green. It was quiet for a very long time.

"Theo?" He looked at me with an unreadable look in his eyes. "I asked that..." I took a deep breath. Why was being honest so hard? I didn't want him to shut down this very deep desire to be family. Kids included. "I want to know what you think."

He chewed his steak slowly. Under other circumstances his barbequed, melt-in-your-mouth steak would have been misjudged as tough. "Well. You really want to know?"

127

I shrugged. And I felt tears sting the back of my eyes. Damn. This was really uncomfortable. I went back to sorting peas.

"When you asked that, and I thought you might be... I felt excited. Now I'm disappointed that you aren't. And I'm just trying to work that all out. Didn't expect that."

I looked up. "You were excited that you thought I might be? Really?"

"Yeah. I'm not your ex, Tess. That would be incredible."

"And you're disappointed that I'm not?"

"Well, yeah. Know the timing wouldn't be great before a wedding and all... but huh, I was."

"You said that your Mum was disappointed that she never got to be a grandmother. You said you didn't want kids."

"Yeah she was disappointed... but that was... Di couldn't have kids after her accident. We didn't go down the IVF track because she'd had enough of doctor's prodding and poking during her rehab. Perhaps that was why the career trajectory was such a big deal for her. I don't blame her really. Not now."

I couldn't hold in my smile. I cut off a piece my steak and ate it enthusiastically.

"You look kind of pleased that my marriage was loaded with tragedy."

"You are okay with kids. That is such a relief. I was terrified it wasn't part of your ten-year plan."

"Tess... I used to have very set ideas about what would be and what would happen. I would love kids to be part of what we get to do together. Very much. But sometimes things don't go according to plan, that's all."

"I get so impatient. I want it all now."

"You want it all now? I think I don't want to wish away what we have right now, for what's coming up next. It will get here when it gets here."

That night as Theo drove off down the track, I lingered outside and watched the silver light of the moon quietly rest on the undulating paddocks. I imagined the Petrea Downs' grave plot on the hill tended and tidy and peaceful. A garden around one particular headstone with just three words, "Faith, Hope, Love" was shining in the moonlight.

I woke up and lay quietly looking into the dark shadows of the pre-dawn morning. I had a lingering sense of profound joy as I had found myself in the room where Meg lay panting as a cry split the air. The midwife wrapped the slippery bundle, and then tied the cord and snipped him free, marking him for independent life. She wiped his eyes with a soft cloth, vernix thick around his scalp. I stood up and retreated to the corner of the room. I was witnessing a most intimate moment. It took my breath away. A family was born. Ben reached out and held his son. A boy. He was perfect. He screwed up his face and bellowed his welcome to the world. I sat down in the corner and cried and cried. Tears of joy.

When I rolled over my pillow was wet.

17.

I walked down the aisle of the Church: flowers, and soft tulle, and petals creating a path towards the altar, directing me forward. Theo turned and our eyes connected. I swallowed back tears. I didn't want my makeup to run. Not today. Sam smiled encouragingly and his mellow voice spoke out, celebrating the acknowledgement that God was here to join with the other witnesses as we sealed our vows. There were no horrible falls, no lost rings, no ripped bridesmaids' dresses, no fainting grooms, no misspelt entries in the registry. It was a beautiful day, a beautiful venue, shared with beautiful friends.

Afterwards, we smiled through the myriad of photographs and enjoyed Ramon's superb catering under a ceiling of fairy lights and stars out in the garden courtyard of the pub. We cut the cake and danced our first dance. We tossed the bouquet. It seemed there was not one tradition that had fallen by the wayside.

And as we said goodbye at the close of the day, I sighed a deep-seated sigh. How perfect. How exhausting. Theo took my hand and opened the door to the car; with assurances it was only a short drive to our stay-over accommodation. His one undisclosed detail was where we would spend our wedding night before we left for our honeymoon. Theo's choice. He insisted I had enough to think about. I had packed up the cottage and moved my things into Theo's place... our place. I had set up the church and decorated the courtyard as our reception venue; calmed and organised Joanie who in the end became quite panicked by the responsibility of details. The week had been a timeline that came down to the wire, synchronised like a well-choreographed dance.

When Theo turned into the Rocky Creek driveway, I started to cry. Theo pulled up outside the stone cottage and slowly drew on the handbrake. "Hey? Did I mess up? Is this not okay?"

I tried to speak, but I just sort of shuddered through my sobs. My makeup started to run. Theo reached over and put his arm around me.

"My bad. I thought Meg and Ben would like to know we spent our first night here as husband and wife."

"This is… perfect. Absolutely perfect."

He made a kind of nervous chuckle. "This is the place that brought us together. It is… where we first kissed. It is where we had our first fight… and where made up."

He came around and opened the door. He led me across the cobble stone path. I saw candles flickering inside. Everything that I left scrubbed and stripped bare at the beginning of the week, was now coordinated and luxurious like a magazine lift out. There was a cute little kitchen installed. They had soft linen and towels on the bed; rugs on the floor; cushions on the lounge; flowers and a bottle of chilled Champaign on the coffee table; chocolates on our pillows; and a generous breakfast hamper in a wicker basket on the bench. Ray and Sandra had worked over and above to have this looking like a dream for us.

"Oh my… the writer's retreat." The basic little shack they let to me when I came was transformed into their beautiful B&B. "It's done. Complete. It is absolutely perfect."

"You look perfect. Are you happy?"

131

"Blissfully. It has been a wonderful day. Thank you."

Theo went and picked up the champaign bottle and popped the cork. I brought two glasses over to him. "To my bride... Mrs Tess Delacey. That has a nice ring."

"And my husband... Oh." I stopped and frowned.

"What?"

"What you said before... How do you know about Meg and Ben?"

"Yikes!"

"You have been snooping! You know about them!"

"I wanted to see what had you so captivated."

"Jealous?"

"Maybe a bit jealous. Got a thumb drive. Stole the file. Read it at work when I was supposed to be doing accounts. I get it actually... why you said you liked visiting with them. Is he patterned after me?"

"Seriously? You think you are Ben?"

"Huh. I guess not then. I do wonder though... I just..."

"Just wondering what?" Everyone's a critic.

"Well, when I read your story, I was just wondering about Ben's mum. I was interested in how you saw her story."

"Elizabeth Perkins'? But that is going backwards to the previous generation." How would that work?

Theo shrugged. He assured me that the precedent made by George Lucas telling the Star Wars back-story out of sequence made it a very acceptable approach.

I was suddenly assailed by questions. If my reader already knew the sad ending of Elizabeth Perkins story, would they want to know more? But then Theo asked that exact question. Perhaps there was enough to tell her story after all. I could edit out some details so that there were large chunks of it left untold. How would Elizabeth cope, going from local sweetheart in school to being scorned and rejected and defiled?

Theo took the glass from my hand and drew me in for a kiss. "Perhaps I shouldn't have brought that up. I'm guessing that is a story for another day."

I looked up at him and smiled, held in his embrace. "Theo?"

"Hmm…"

"I'm so grateful I get to do life with you. Thank you." My makeup started to run again.

He grabbed a tissue from the box on the sideboard and blotted my face. "Content, my little fiction-writer?"

I nodded. I looked around this little retreat that had introduced me to stories of life, of healing and hope. Each stone built on the next to create a place of restoration in the face of painful life experiences. Some stories are adventurous, some are happily ever after, and some stories contain enough hope to be considered not very good reading. I smiled and thought that was my story. Yet it was also the grander story because I was living it… and as I raised my glass, I smiled knowing there is still much more of our story to be lived… and to be told. And I couldn't wait to start.

The End

More Stories by Olwyn Harris

Houses of Healing Series

#1 The Beachside Cottage

Eliza-Beth finds herself being disowned by her family and in danger of being sent to the poorhouse. Jensen, whose heart is still broken by the sudden death of his wife, meets Eliza-Beth on a dark night and devises a plan to rescue her from her inpending doom. The journey they enbark on leads them to where neither of them expected to end up.

#2 Petrea Downs

The death of her husband leaves Meg struggling to keep the farm going on her own. When she shoots a stranger who is trying to steal her cattle and is required to nurse him back to health, she has no idea that Ben Harker is going to be the salve needed for healing her own deep-seated wounds of grief.

Gems of Australia: 6 Part Faith Series

#1 Sapphires of Hope

A tacky basket that is the only thing available for Andi to use as for her catering assignment reveals some interesting pieces of historical information. In order to try and understand what they mean, Jo and Andi visit the farm where the basket came from with June, a distant family member, but find themselves in the circumstances that almost cost Andi her life and almost distroyed the livihood of the family living at the time of our Federation. Jo learns that having hope enables people to keep going even when things are beyond your control.

Stand-Alone Stories

Matt's Boys of Wattle Creek.

When Matthew Lawson's three sons were born, he wrote each of them a letter outlining his hopes and prayers for their futures. When he decided to give up his city job and move to the little town of Wattle Creek, he could never have imagined the effect it would have on his young family. As Matt's boys grow to maturity and find their places in their community, will his dreams and prayers come to fulfilment? Will his boys develop their own faith in the eternal God? And will they each find the kind of love that Matt holds for his beautiful Josie?

Maggie & Minatour

Another great book by this author. Maggie & Minotaur is a conflict-filled journey to the earlier days of Australia's colonisation. A time when racism and classism was rampant. This book uses historically accurate and yet, very confrontational language, especially around the issue of race, words we don't use in polite society these days. It paints an accurate - if unflattering - picture of early life in Australia.

All that aside, however, this book takes you into the home and lives of a very culturally diverse society trying to come to terms with the changing expectations of the time, woven through with wonderful characters, loving relationships, and the ever-present grace of God. Olwyn Harris knows how to tell a story and this book is no exception!

Coming Soon from Olwyn Harris

Gems of Australia: 6 Part Faith Series

#2 Rubies of Ambition
Jo and Andi travel back in time again with an acttress from the 1920's in order to help her reconnect with the people in her town. The catus plague is at its height and the desperation of the people is felt on all levels.

#3 Emereld Dreams
Another journey finds Jo and Andi back in colonial times and they are horrified at the living conditions of most of those who had no choice but the live in Australia.

Children's Stories

Bush Olympics
A great story that helps children understand that they are uniquie in God's sight and that if they work with the skills that He has given them they will be able to work as part of a team to achieve great things.

www.ingramcontent.com/pod-product-compliance
Lightning Source LLC
Chambersburg PA
CBHW030435120726
47903CB00003B/974